Critical acclaim for Darklands

'All the pros and cons of contemporary horror fiction are distilled in this slim but valuable volume. The pros are short stories – by established writers such as Stephen Gallagher and Derek Marlowe, and by interesting newcomers such as Julie Akhurst and Michael Marshall Smith – which do not slot easily into any pigeonhole, except that they are all extremely disturbing. . . . This is an excellent collection. Smith's story, in particular, is a *tour de force*'

The Times

' . . . The quality the collection exudes the most is paranoia. The stories mostly feature people on a downward spiral of sanity, with differing results. It's a good collection, and well worth a look'

Starburst

'In recent years horror fiction has become increasingly flexible and sophisticated, trends which are admirably illustrated in this remarkable little anthology of original stories. . . . The contributors range from established authors such as Stephen Gallagher and boy-wonder Mark Morris to new writers, including Julie Akhurst whose *Small Pieces of Alice* is one of the most chilling, deadly stories in the collection. Alan David Price contributes a tear-jerking urban apocalypse tale and Joel Lane's *Common Land* provides an unforgettable image of blighted lives. All in all *Darklands* has certainly earned a place in the shadows of your library, where the candles burn low, it's always past midnight and all the books breathe menace . . .'

City Limits

'Surreal fantasy, dark fantasy, weird tales. . . . The dark lands are really inside ourselves, working on our imaginations, the bit that sees the lord of the flies nailed to the front door when we go down to collect the mail . . . There isn't a weak 'un here. Like Nick Royle says, don't read it with the lights out, you won't see anything'

Vector

'*Darklands* is a cutting edge anthology of new British horror writing. Contributors include Stephen Gallagher and Derek Marlowe, most are under 30 and see horror writing not as escapism but as bloody psychological realism'

The Good Times

About the editor

Nicholas Royle was born in Sale, Cheshire, in 1963. He graduated in modern languages from the University of London, then combined writing with a series of full-time jobs for six years before going freelance in 1992. He has had more than sixty short stories published in anthologies and magazines both in the UK and abroad, including *Cutting Edge, Interzone, Fiction Magazine, The Fred, The Year's Best Horror Stories, Best New Horror, In Dreams, The Sun Rises Red, Sugar Sleep, Dark Voices,* and many more.

His work has been nominated twice for Best Short Story in the British Fantasy Awards and in 1992 he received the Best Anthology Award for *Darklands*.

His first novel, *Counterparts*, is published by Barrington Books.

DARKLANDS

---

edited by Nicholas Royle

**with a foreword by
Ramsey Campbell**

NEW ENGLISH LIBRARY

Hodder and Stoughton

Copyright remains with contributors.
Foreword © Ramsey Campbell.
Introduction © Nicholas Royle.

First published in Great Britain in 1991 by Egerton Press

New English Library paperback edition 1993

British Library C.I.P.
A CIP Catalogue record for this title is available from the British Library

ISBN 0 450 59764 4

The right of the contributors to be identified as the authors of this work has been asserted by them in accordance with the Copyright, Designs and Patents Act 1988.

Typeset on the Apple™ System using Quark Xpress™ by the editor.

Printed and bound in Great Britain for Hodder and Stoughton Paperbacks, a division of Hodder and Stoughton Ltd, Mill Road, Dunton Green, Sevenoaks, Kent TN13 2YA (Editorial Office: 47 Bedford Square, London WC1B 3DP) by Cox & Wyman Limited, Reading. Typeset by Hewer Text Composition Services, Edinburgh.

contents

With thanks to JA, MA, JB, JRC, CG, GK, CM, GM, KN, MS, LT, IW, the BFS, David Almond, Chris Reed, Nick Summers, David J Tomlinson, Di Wathen, and all the contributors. Thanks to MSA for technical support.

FOREWORD

This is a remarkable anthology – in some ways too remarkable for its own good. I mean that comment to express both my enthusiasm for the book and my dismay at the apparent state of the present market for anthologies. Nick Royle has had the temerity to put together a book of tales of, on the whole, the macabre which are not easily categorised, and for two years he has shown it to all the likely publishers. It seems that despite the lineup of fiction and contributors, which (while the book was being shown around) also included Kim Newman and myself, publishers don't feel they can take a risk with a book so strange.

Once they would have. Neither John Gawsworth nor the *Evening Standard* appear to have had much trouble in the thirties in getting fat strange anthologies into print, and indeed Herbert van Thal did well with *A Book of Strange Stories* in his more tasteful days. Gone for the nonce are the days when Marjorie Bowen could subtitle *More Great Tales of Horror* (1935) as 'a collection of strange stories of amazement, horror and wonder'. Or perhaps, happily, they are back again, because I think the above would be no bad subtitle for Nick Royle's book.

At any rate, it might cover the considerable range of fiction Nick has chosen, all the way from the subtle ghostliness of Stephen Gallagher's tale to Alan David

9

Price's lyrical improvisation on a monumental theme. Quite a few of the stories deal or may deal with the dark places of the mind, but in how many different ways: Julie Akhurst's sinuous paranoia, Kevin Mullins' hereditary nightmare, Philip Nutman's replication of the voice of a mind drawing in its limits. Judy Hines tells a conte cruel, and Derek Marlowe recounts a piercingly sad tale which we all may know. Brian Howell transmutes depersonalisation into art, while Joel Lane makes manifest an occult vision of urban alienation. Mark Morris's piece may lead the reader to believe it intends to be a horror story, but it leads to a surreal revelation. As for Michael Marshall Smith's tale, I don't know if it is surrealism or horror fiction, or entirely possibly both, but it is the purest nightmare: a story (by no means the only one within) which I should be proud to have written myself.

In recent years too much of the field of the macabre has been dominated by the crude and cheap and exploitative, not to mention a good deal of bloody awful prose which it would be overly kind to describe as semi-literate. Fiction such as you now hold in your hands, and as much of it as possible, is a heartening answer to this problem. If this book can see print only as a privately published volume, then at least that's a start. I hope it is now on its way to reaching the wide audience which it deserves.

Ramsey Campbell
Wallasey, 11 October 1991

INTRODUCTION TO THE NEW EDITION

When *Darklands* first appeared in November 1991, Ramsey Campbell's characteristically generous foreword described the circumstances surrounding its publication. Unable to sell the book, I'd set up my own imprint – Egerton Press – and published a limited edition of 500 copies.

I conceived the idea for the anthology in 1987: to publish original work by new and unpublished writers alongside new stories by some of the great names of the British horror/fantasy tradition. John Burke, whose *Tales of Unease* anthologies – along with Ramsey Campbell's *New Terrors* volumes – had influenced my thinking, provided much early encouragement and advice. I approached half a dozen major publishers, in turn, with the anthology. The kindest offer I received was for lunch.

Obviously, I went for lunch, and it was very good too, but by the time the After Eight wrappers had been folded a hundred different ways, the writers I'd got lined up in the anthology were no nearer seeing their work in print. Some were veterans and their patience was extraordinary. Most of the new writers, to whom I'd offered huge exposure and great wealth, no doubt deciphered the wretched signature of destiny in this series of delays; the inevitable abandonment of the project was constantly being deferred.

Then, in June 1989, I signed an unusual pre-contract contract with an independent publisher. For certain odd reasons, the manuscript was rejected a year later, and so I started again, cold-calling on publishers and seeing the lights in their eyes go out as soon as they heard the word 'anthology' – it was like watching an office building close down for the night.

All around me, however, anthologies were being bought up from the US. Collections of horror stories about sex, vampires and . . . *architecture*. Even original British collections were breaking through, as long as they were about popular music or psychic superheroes. 'What's the theme?' a publisher would ask. 'Well, there isn't one. It's just a bunch of excellent stories.' 'Hmm. Have you tried the *Writers' and Artists' Yearbook*?'

By July 1991 I'd approached seventeen publishers and it began to dawn on me that I might not sell *Darklands*, after all. So, either I abandoned the book or I published it myself. How could I make the decision?

Tails.

I'd already lost one or two of the professionals' stories as other deadlines had come around. I returned a few more stories to writers whom I felt I couldn't ask if I might use their work for free. (Most later indicated they would have been glad to let me.) I set up Egerton Press and published the book on November 14, 1991, to coincide with the British Fantasy Convention.

A sixth of the print run sold over the first weekend. Excellent reviews appeared in *The Times, City Limits, Million, Starburst* and other journals. One year on, *Darklands* picked up the British Fantasy Award for Best Anthology, beating several big commercial anthologies on the way. Two stories from the collection were nominated for the Best Short Story award – Michael Marshall Smith's *The Dark Land* and Julie Akhurst's *Small Pieces of Alice* – and Smith's won it. His story was reprinted in *Best New Horror 3* (Robinson) edited by Stephen Jones and Ramsey Campbell, while Joel Lane's *Common Land* went into Karl Wagner's *The Year's Best Horror Stories XX*. Stephen Gallagher's *The Visitors' Book* was reprinted twice, in

Ellen Datlow and Terri Windling's *The Year's Best Fantasy & Horror* and Heinemann's *Best Short Stories 1992* edited by Giles Gordon and John Hughes, *and* read out abridged on Radio 4.

With the exception of this introduction, the anthology is reprinted here in its original form. The stories explore the darklands of the heart and the mind: the personal darklands of eleven very different writers treading the line between night and day. Unconstrained by a common theme, they share a readiness to say 'what if . . .', to investigate the dark side of our emotional and psychological experience.

There are several new writers. Julie Akhurst, Judy Hines, Brian Howell, Kevin Mullins and Alan David Price are all names which are new to the field. Joel Lane, Mark Morris, Philip Nutman and Michael Marshall Smith are already rising stars; while Stephen Gallagher and Derek Marlowe have many novels and screen projects both behind them and to come.

'Why do you write this stuff?' ask some, assuming that horror stories don't address the same themes as mainstream fiction. But they do. The good ones do. They deal with the same matters as arise in all good fiction: people, relationships, love, fear, mortality, identity, hopes, disappointments, dreams, nightmares. The same things we deal with every day of our lives.

But they *are* stories of horror and fantasy. They are dark. The ways in which these writers work are unsettling and disturbing, sometimes actually – really – frightening.

At this point, tradition suggests I should advise you not to read these stories: before going to sleep/when alone in the house/before a dental appointment/at all if of a nervous disposition, etc. I would add: don't read them with the lights off. You won't get very far.

Maybe you should read them in the way they were written – one at a time, in a room on your own – in order to appreciate them fully. Allow these writers to lead you into their own personal darklands. You may find that you share some common ground with them. You may even find it difficult to leave. Especially if you are about to go to sleep.

And the name of the publisher that invited me to lunch all those years ago? New English Library, of course.

Nicholas Royle
London, 1 February 1993

The visitors' book

Stephen Gallagher

Stephen Gallagher was born in October 1954 in Salford, Lancashire. After graduating in drama and English from Hull University he went to work as a researcher for Yorkshire Television and later moved to Granada. He began writing in 1977 and made his first professional sale a year later. The author of nine novels – The Last Rose of Summer/Dying of Paradise, The Ice Belt, Chimera, Follower, Valley of Lights, Oktober, Down River, Rain *and* The Boat House *– he has also worked extensively in radio and television, adapting his own fiction and scripting two series of* Doctor Who. *A four-part serial adapted from* Chimera *was broadcast on ITV in July 1991. Other screen projects include* Valley of Lights, Oktober, Down River *and* The Horn. *His next novel, due in 1992, will be* Nightmare, With Angel.

He has written more than 20 short stories for F&SF, Shadows, Winter Chills, New Crimes, Dark Fantasies, *and* Arrows of Eros, *among others.*

Stephen Gallagher lives with his wife and young daughter in the Ribble Valley near Blackburn. When he's not writing, he's feeling guilty about not writing. 'The free-floating anxieties in our minds,' he says of The Visitors' Book, *'are always looking for something in the outside world to hang themselves upon.' The following story illustrates his theory of what horror fiction is all about: 'The restless human need to work up solid metaphors for unformed anxieties . . . they give us some dim but definite sense of the awesome nature of our inner landscape.'*

The visitors' book

'Someone's torn a page out of this,' she said, turning the book toward me. 'Look, you can see.'

She was almost right. The page hadn't been torn, it had been cut; taken out with a blade that had been run down the middle of the book as close to the centre as it was possible to get. It was the kind of cut you make when you don't want your handiwork to be noticed. The only thing that gave it away was that when the book was closed, a slight gap appeared as if a bookmark had been lost in there somewhere. It made me faintly curious, but no more than that. I really didn't think that it was any big deal.

'So it has,' I said, and tried to look more interested than I was.

Some time later, I remember getting it out of the drawer to look at it again. It was a big book, album-sized, and it was two-thirds filled with handwritten entries by many of the families who'd stayed in the summerhouse before us. Only one or two of them were in a language I could understand, and they gave a few hints about the place – how to puzzle out how the circuit breakers worked, where to get English newspapers two days out of date – as well as the standard, had-a-lovely-time kinds of sentiments. There were some people from Newcastle, others who'd come over from Dorset. Many of the others were Germans, a few French. Sally hadn't come across the book until we'd been in the place for three days already, and then she'd found it while rummaging around in the sitting-room furniture for maps and brochures. When I eventually went back and brought it out again, I turned to the place where the missing page had been and looked at the entries before and after. I couldn't remember anything of what had been written, but by then I was only interested in the dates. The gap seemed to correspond to a two-week period exactly one year before.

No, I remember thinking. *It can't have any significance.* All that it probably meant was that someone had messed up their entry and had taken the leaf out to try it again. The paper-cutter they'd used was still there at the back of the drawer, a little plastic block with just the corner of a razor blade showing.

When I turned the paper to the light, I could see that some of the missing writing had pressed through onto the next page. Not to the extent that I could make out any words, but enough to get an idea of the overall style. It was neat, it was rounded. A feminine hand.

And it didn't match with any of the entries that came before or after.

But that was later. Back on that third day, there was no reason for the Visitors' Book to bother me at all. I left Sally looking through the remaining pages, and went out onto the covered terrace on the front of the summerhouse.

'Watcha doing, Minx?' I said.

The Minx looked up at me from the table. On her birth certificate and by her grandparents she was called Victoria, but to us she'd been the Minx for so long that we had to make an effort to remember that she had any other name. She was four years old that autumn, and was due to start at school the following spring. She'd have her own books, nametabs, a uniform, everything. We'd always told ourselves that we could look forward to this – like all children she'd hit our lives like a hurricane, leaving us dazed and off-kilter and somehow feeling that we'd never quite be able to make up the ground again to become the people we'd once been – but I found that I wasn't quite anticipating the event in the way that I'd imagined. I suppose I was just beginning to realise how closely the growing and the going away were entwined, and would ever be so.

'I'm colouring,' she said.

She was, too. She'd coloured the page in her book and a good piece of the old vinyl tablecloth around it. She'd coloured a cow blue, and the sky behind it black.

I said, 'That looks really good. Are you going to do another?'

'I'll do another next Tuesday,' she said, Next Tuesday being her way of indicating some undetermined time in the future. 'Let's go and look for froggies.'

'Clear your lunch away first,' I said, 'or you'll bring in all kinds of creepy-crawlies.'

She climbed down from the bench to the wooden planking of the terrace, and surprised me by doing what I'd asked of her. Then we set off down the steps and into the grounds to find some froggies.

It was a pretty good house. I'd felt a twinge of disappointment when we'd first rolled up the grassy drive after a long haul by road and ferry, but within a few hours of unpacking and beginning to unwind it had started to grow on me. It was bigger than we needed, but I liked the sense of space. So what if it was a little shabby round the edges and the shower arrangements were kind of spartan and the beds were dropped in the middle in a way that would have suited a hunchback perfectly and nobody else at all; after a while this only seemed to add to the atmosphere.

It was late, a quiet time of the year. Almost all of the other summerhouses, including the newer one that shared this grassy clearing in a thicket just a little way back from the beach, appeared to be unoccupied. When the road gate at the end of the driveway was closed, it was almost as if we were shutting ourselves into a private world. When the Minx had spotted the horde of tiny frogs that seemed to migrate across the drive at around four o'clock every

afternoon, that more or less confirmed it. It seemed that
we were going to be okay.

'Have you found any?' she asked brightly, but I had
to tell her that I hadn't. She liked to hold them on her
hand. By now they probably just sat there toughing it
out and thinking, *Oh, shit, not again* and *Why me, God,
why me?*

'No,' I said. 'It's the wrong time of day. Look, I saw a
bike in the garage yesterday. Why don't you ride it around
the garden?'

'A big bike?' she said warily.

'No, just a little bike.'

So we spent the afternoon playing with the house's rusty
old tricycle and a football that we'd picked up from Willi's
Market about a half-mile down the shore road, and after
we'd eaten picnic-style out on the terrace we all took a
walk along the beach until it was too cold for everybody
but the Minx, who had to be picked up out of the sandhole
that she'd dug and carried home squalling.

And as we were tracing our way back through the
upturned boats and then across the strip of coarse grass-
land that divided the shoreline from the shore road,
I found myself thinking: *Maybe the people who wrote
the page weren't the ones who took it out. Maybe it
was something that the owners didn't want the rest of
us to see.*

The owners.

Those shadowy people who weren't actually present
but whose mark was everywhere, so that they seemed
to stand just out of sight like a bunch of watchful ghosts.
Their pictures, their ornaments, their old castoff furniture
– their house. Maybe they came in after each new tenant
and read the book, and there was something here that
they'd censored.

Maybe.

Exactly what I had in mind, I couldn't have said.
Something uncomplimentary, some insult even; written
by someone who perhaps didn't have a good time and

blamed the place and not themselves for it. Or worse. It could have been something worse. I was surprised to find that the possibility had been playing on my mind. I said nothing to Sally, but I decided there and then that I'd think about it no further. I mean, you worry at something to which you know you can never find the answer, and where does it get you?

Nowhere. So I thought I'd better stop.

That night, after the Minx had been installed in her room and had exhausted every avenue for stories and drinks and had eventually exhausted herself as well, we got a couple of the local beers out of the fridge and turned on the sitting-room lights. Sally flicked through some of the magazines that she'd picked up on the boat coming over, and I hunted around for the paperback I'd been reading. I'm not much of a reader, and thinking of the two weeks that lay ahead I'd bought the book for its size and weight as much as for any other reason. Every other page was dotted with CIA and MI5 and KGB, and the plot went on and on and had about as much grip as a wet handshake; after a while I gave up looking for it, and went over to the shelves instead.

There had to be something here I could read. There was a cabinet full of books and overseas editions of the *Reader's Digest*, most of them probably abandoned and accumulated from visitors over the years, but there wasn't much that was in the English language. There was a fat book by Leon Uris that I put back because it looked such heavy going and, besides, I'd already seen the movie, and an old and brittle Agatha Christie which, on a quick check, appeared to have lost its last ten pages. The only decent bet seemed to be a two-fisted private eye story titled *Dames Die First*.

When I pulled it out, a photograph dropped to the floor. It had been between the books. I picked it up and looked at it, and saw that there was the sign of a crease across the middle. At a guess, it had been slipped in between the volumes for the pressure to flatten it out, and then it had been forgotten. It was of a blonde girl of about six or seven, and if it had been taken anywhere around here I didn't recognise the spot. I carried the picture over to the chest of drawers and then started to go through them, much as Sally had earlier in the day. After a while I became aware of her watching me.

'What's the matter?' she said.

'Just checking on something.'

She didn't seem to think much of my answer, but it was the best one I had. As she was laying down her magazine to come over, I found what I was looking for; another, different photograph that lay in one of the drawers underneath some boxed games and out-of-date timetables.

It was a family group. Nothing formal, just a snapshot. The house was recognisable in the background, although they'd added to it since. These, I'd been guessing, were the people who actually owned the place and who let it out through an agency for the times when they didn't need it themselves.

I laid the two photographs side by side on top of the dresser. The girl who appeared in one didn't appear in the other.

Sally picked up the portrait shot and said, 'She doesn't look local,' before dropping it again and going on through the kitchen toward the bathroom.

Yeah, fine.

That's probably what I'd been thinking, too.

Saturday came around.

I didn't actually realise that it was Saturday until I saw a strange car coming up the driveway that morning. At first I thought that it was somebody on their way to speak to us, but the car turned off and pulled in by the other of the two houses that shared the driveway and the private clearing at its end. Suddenly it didn't seem so private any more.

The family got out and we nodded to each other. They didn't seem to have brought much in the way of luggage and they went straight into the house as if they already knew their way around. My guess was that they were another set of owners, just up for the weekend. I went back into our own place and warned Sally and the Minx, just in case either of them happened to be wandering around after a shower in less than their underwear. There was just a stretch of open ground between the two buildings, nothing screening them at all. The other house was newer, neater. I know it was theirs, but I couldn't help thinking of them as intruders.

I looked at the two children. Neither of them was anything like the girl in the photograph.

So then I wondered if they might be able to tell me what had happened here, in this same week exactly one year before.

But I never asked.

On Sunday we took the Minx on a long drive to the zoo, where she acted up so much that we had to threaten to leave her there and halfway meant it. When we got back late in the afternoon, our short-term neighbours were apparently loading up to go. We nodded as we passed just as before, and then they went.

I gave it a few minutes after their departure and then I took a walk down the driveway to check that the gate was secure; the driveway curved and was lined with dense bushes, so the gate couldn't be seen directly from the house. The Minx came after me, on the prospect of froggies. She squatted down looking hopefully at the ground while I rattled the wide gate, but the bolt was secure.

'Why are you doing that?' she said.

'So that we can let you wander around without worrying about you getting onto the road where the cars are,' I told her. 'Haven't you noticed how one of us checks on it every morning?'

'I check on it too,' she said.

'Really.'

'Yes,' she said. 'Someone keeps coming in and leaving it open.'

Either the frogs had already been and gone, or else they were getting wiser and waiting. We walked back up to the house. The day was dying and the shadows were long and deep, and the houselights glowed yellow-on-blue like a twilit jack-o'-lantern. The Minx took hold of my hand as we climbed the wooden steps. Only a couple of hours before, she'd been winding me up to bursting point outside the monkey house and she'd known it. Now this. I couldn't help thinking, and not for the first time, that the worst thing in the world for me would be to lose her.

And, of course, eventually to lose her was one of the few things in my life that could fairly be called inevitable.

With only a few days left of our stay, we found ourselves less inclined toward loading up the car and going looking for late-season amusements and so instead we just stayed around the place. I'm not exactly sure what we did, but the time carried on leaking away from us anyway. Anything we needed, we could usually get it from Willi's Market. The only problem was that we couldn't mention the name of the place when the Minx was in earshot without her latching onto it and getting us helpless with laughter.

Sometimes the Minx walked down with me. Thursday was one of the days when she didn't.

It was a rambling, one-storey building set back from the road with space for about half a dozen cars in front of it, and although it wasn't big it sold just about everything from fresh bread to padlocks. It was clean and it was bright and it was modern, and the only note that jarred when I compared it to similar places back home was the sales rack of shrink-wrapped pornography stuck in there by the checkout between the Disney comics and the chewing gum. One man seemed to run the place on his own, at least at this quiet time of year when there were only the few locals and late visitors like ourselves to keep it ticking over. He wore a sports shirt and glasses and combed his thinning hair straight back, and whenever I went in we communicated entirely by nods and signs and smiles.

As he was punching up my stuff on the till, I brought out the little girl's picture and showed it to him.

He paused in his work and looked at the picture. He wasn't certain of why I was doing this, and so he looked closely without any reaction other than mild puzzlement for a few moments. Then he glanced up at me.

He shook his head. There was sadness and sympathy in his eyes.

And he said something, and right there and then I'd have given almost anything to know what it was; but I just took the picture from him and stowed it away again, and I nodded my head as if I understood. The words meant nothing to me, but I thought I knew the tone of them.

It was the tone, I believed then, that one would use when speaking of someone else's tragedy.

As I was walking back along the side of the shore road, I felt as if the formless apprehensions of the past few days had suddenly come together and made a creature with a name. Its name was dread, and it sat in me like an angry prisoner with no sight of daylight. A few cars zipped by me, one with a windsurfing board on its rack. I knew I'd closed and bolted the gate behind me, I *knew* it, and yet . . .

In my mind's eye I could see the Minx running hell-for-leather down the drive, giggling in mischief the way she often did, with Sally screaming a warning and falling behind and the Minx too giddy to realise what she was being told . . . *Someone keeps coming in and leaving it open*, she'd said, and I'd paid her no attention . . .

But who? Apart from our weekend neighbours, we were the only ones to be using the gateway at all. *Was* there someone who'd been prowling around the place, and I'd overlooked the evidence because it was the Minx who was telling me and I was so used to the workings of her imagination that I was dismissing the truth along with the usual dose of unreality?

Come to think of it, the garage door had been standing open when we'd gone to get the bike a few days before.

And I still hadn't found that damned paperback, even though I was pretty sure of where I'd left it.

And there was the Visitors' Book, which had planted the seed of my unease.

And the reaction of the checkout man in Willi's Market, that had brought it into flower . . .

Pretty thin fabric, I know.

But by the time I reached the house I was running.

Sally saw me coming up the drive. I must have been a sight. Breathless, my shirt half-out, the bag of groceries crushed up against my side. She was out on a sun lounger in front of the house, and she raised her head and squinted at me. I slowed. Everything seemed normal, and I was a dope. But I wasn't sorry.

'Where's the Minx?' I said.

'She's set herself up with a picnic on the porch,' she said. 'What's the matter with *you*?'

'Nothing,' I said, almost sharply, and I walked past her and up the steps to the covered entrance. As my eyes adjusted to the shade, I could see the Minx; in a world of her own as she so often was, with plates and crockery from the kitchen set out on the outdoor dining table and her all-time favourite doll, clothes long gone and the rest of her distinctly frayed around the edges, propped up outside. She'd hijacked the big tub of margarine and a packet of biscuits, and Sally must have opened a bottle of cola for her to round off the feast. She was just raising it to her lips and tilting it as I came into sight.

Nothing amiss here.

And then, in an instant, I saw that I was wrong.

I don't know exactly what happens when you're in a situation like that. You can see the most minor detail with the utmost clarity, and it burns itself deep into your awareness; but it's almost as if the sheer volume of information suddenly slows the speed of processing, so that you don't seem to act or react in any positive way at all. You see your own failure, even before it's had the chance to happen. Disaster's heading straight for you like a rocket, and your responses are moving like letters in the mail.

If I had any talent with a paintbrush, I could probably reproduce the scene exactly. The well-worn sheen on the checkered vinyl cloth. The sunlight, backlighting the Minx's hair as she raised the bottle. The mismatched china and the scattering of crumbs. The open margarine tub, its contents churned like an angry sea. The last inch of flat cola.

And the live wasp in the bottle, floating toward the neck as the bottle was tilted.

She screamed and dropped the bottle, and clapped both her hands to her face. The wasp was on the deckboards now, buzzing furiously but too wet or too damaged to rise; she'd squeezed it between her mouth and the rim of the bottle as it had tried to escape, and it had reacted the only way it knew how. Which got no sympathy out of me at all. I stepped on it quickly, and it popped like a grape.

The Minx was still screaming as I hauled her up and onto my knee. Sally was already on her way up the steps. I tried to pull the Minx's hands away, but she was hysterical. Sally was saying 'What is it, what's happened?' and I remember thinking, completely unfairly but in the lashout, bite-anything manner of a run-over dog, that she should have been right there and this should never have been allowed to happen. Which makes no sense, of course, but that's the way I was thinking. I don't think it showed on the outside, but I was in a panic. I didn't know what to do. We were in the middle of nowhere in a place where we didn't speak the language, and there was a crisis here and I *didn't know what to do*.

The stinger was still in the Minx's lip, like a tiny yellow thumbtack. I managed to pick it out carefully with my thumbnail. And what then? I tried to have a go at sucking out the poison, but the Minx beat me away. Sally ran to the kitchen and brought back half an onion to rub the wound, but the Minx batted that away too. She was screaming for a plaster, the little-kids' answer to every hurt. I handed her over and went for the first-aid kit in the car.

There were Band-aids, there were bandages, there was a folded-up sling for a broken arm. I'd bought the kit as a ready-made box and I don't think I'd even looked into it since I'd taken a curious glance over the contents and then stowed it away in the car at least three years before. I fumbled it, and the contents went everywhere. I saw some antiseptic wipes and grabbed one up and went back to the covered terrace.

The Minx, still tearful, was quieter. Sally was rocking her and whispering *Sshh, sshh*, and the Minx was sobbing. I tore open the sachet and crouched down before them both and managed to get a few dabs in with the wipe. Her lip was already beginning to swell.

I was scared.

When the swelling grew steadily worse over the next half-hour, we loaded her into the car and went out looking for a hospital. I had no idea. We were already on the road and moving when I thought that I should have checked through the old brochures and guides for an area map which might have some indication on it. I had a terrific sense of desperation, as if there were a bomb ticking in the back of the car. I hardly knew what I was doing. In the end it was the cashier at a big Shell service area who marked the nearest hospital on a tourist map and then waved me away when I tried to pay for it.

Carrying the Minx into the Emergency Room, I felt like a wrecked sailor reaching the shore. I mean, for all I knew, she could have *died* – she could have been dying right then, and I'd have been no more useful. As it was they checked her over, gave her a couple of shots, painted the sting site with something, and then sent us away. The Minx stayed quiet in the back with Sally as I drove us all home. It was dusk when we got there, and it was to find that we'd gone off leaving every door and window of the place wide open. Even the gate at the end of the drive was swinging to and fro, and I knew that I'd stopped and jumped out of the car to close it behind us.

I knew that I'd never feel quite the same again, about anything. I'd crossed a line. I'd peeped into the abyss.

Nothing much more happened those last couple of days. I put the child's photograph back on the shelf where I'd found it, and I made no further enquiries. The Minx looked like a defeated boxer, five rounds and then out for the count, but by the next morning we were even able to make jokes about it. They were morale-boosters, not the real thing, and I suppose they must have sounded pretty hollow to both of us. The camera stayed in its case for the rest of the trip. Nothing was said or agreed, but I think that this was something that none of us would ever want to be reminded of.

So, no more photographs.

We'd probably have gone home early if we could, but the boat ticket couldn't be transferred. And, besides, there was so little time remaining. The weather held good, but we stuck around the house killing time as if on the rainiest of rainy days.

On the last day we packed almost in silence, and the Minx went for one last froggie-hunt while I loaded up the car. Sally stayed in the house. When I went inside to bring out the last few items – the boots, the overcoats, the radio . . . all the stuff that didn't belong in any particular box or bag – I found her at the big table in the sitting room. The Visitors' Book was open on the table before her. She looked up, and she seemed almost defensive.

'We've got to write something,' she said. 'It's not the house's fault. Not to put anything at all would be rude.'

I shrugged, and didn't say anything. We hadn't been saying much of anything to each other since the accident, at least not directly. I picked up the stuff that I'd come for and went out to the car.

Half an hour later, with everything loaded away and the

house locked up for the last time behind us, we rolled down the driveway and out through the open gate.

'Say Goodbye, house,' Sally told the Minx, and the Minx turned and waved through the back window and said, 'Bye!'

I stopped the car.

'I just realised, I left my sunglasses,' I said.

'I checked everywhere before we locked up,' Sally said. 'Are you sure?'

'I only meant to put them down for a second,' I said. 'I know where they are. Let me have the keys.'

The keys were to be dropped off at the agents' office in the nearest town as we drove on by to the ferry. Sally got them out of the big envelope and passed them forward to me, and I got out of the car and walked back up the drive. I left the engine running. This wasn't going to take very long.

Already the house seemed different. No longer ours, it was a place of strangers again. I felt out-of-place, almost observed, as I walked up the steps with the door key in my hand. I could hear the car's engine running at the end of the driveway, over on the far side of the bushes.

I entered the newly regained silence of the place. There was no sign of my sunglasses but then, I'd known there wouldn't be; they were in their case, safe inside my jacket.

I didn't have much time. I crossed the room to the chest of drawers and crouched, pulling open the one which I knew held the Visitors' Book. It was uppermost on all the brochures, and I took it out and laid it on top of the chest before feeling around at the back of the drawer. Then I straightened, and opened the book to the latest entry.

I didn't want to read it. In fact I'd turned the book around so that all of the entries were upside-down to me, on purpose. I didn't know whether Sally had mentioned anything about how the visit had ended, and I didn't want to. I spread the pages flat and I took a grip on the little cutter and I ran it, firmly and neatly, down the final page as close to the spine as I could get.

A firm tug, and it came out cleanly. I screwed it up and stuffed it into my pocket, for quiet disposal at a stopover point somewhere on the journey ahead.

And then I closed the book, returned it to the drawer, locked up the house, and walked away.

Forever.

Small pieces of Alice

Julie Akhurst

Julie Akhurst was born in Orsett, Essex, in December 1963. She was the eldest of four children and her father was a clergyman who left the Church of England to become a primary school teacher. She was brought up in Norfolk and taught by both parents while at school. She attended a Norwich comprehensive and won two scholarships to Oxford. After graduating in English she worked as secretary to a publishing director of a small company in Kent, discovering only that she possessed no secretarial ability at all. The Jim Bakker scandal in America meant that charity donations to the parent company of her firm dropped dramatically and she was made redundant as a direct result. She was offered another job, this time with a bestselling monthly magazine. She was promoted from secretary to more important secretary, then to editorial assistant, excerpts editor, sub-editor and finally associate editor. She left to take up the job of deputy features editor on a weekly magazine. She lives and works in London.

While waiting for this anthology to materialise, Julie sold stories to H *and* Skeleton Crew, *but both magazines folded before her stories appeared, which means that* Small Pieces of Alice *is still her first published short story. It's a brilliantly assured and unsettling debut.*

Small pieces of Alice

Emilia took off her spectacles and rubbed the thin skin of her eyelids and across the bridge of her nose. Then she replaced her spectacles, blinked sharply and shook back her hair. She was beginning to see the dead animals again.

Of course they weren't there when she swallowed down her fear and walked up to them. The splayed, broken form of a rabbit was one of those small weighted sacks used inexplicably wherever men were working on the road; or she was staring at a flapping piece of newspaper when she had seen a dying gull beating its wings senselessly against a lamppost. She always did ask herself what such a proliferation of carelessly squandered wildlife would be doing in W2, but it was a question without the conviction that it had any right to be asked, used in the face of blind panic like a parasol against the mugger's knife.

She put her chin down now and walked firmly up to the dead collie whose blood-stained fur was twitching in the breeze; and it happily resolved itself into an oddly-coloured corner of the shop wall, the tattered remnant of a handkerchief. Slowly she let out a shuddering sigh, pretending even to herself that nothing had unnerved her. She had already walked on, her small, firm footsteps ringing up the hard pavement of the Bayswater Road.

Last night she had seen Nell in silhouette in her darkened office, the huge outline of her stomach standing out against the little light that filtered through the window blind. Her head was thrown back so that the fall of her hair slid over the desk and just touched the ground. She should have been a Madonna with that expression on her face. There was a quattrocento serenity in the curve of her lip, the downcast eyelid, that would have spoken of a secret and holy communion with the child within her if it had been found on any bas-relief – or on anybody but Nell. Emilia's stomach turned as she followed once more in her mind the shadowy arch that began with Nell's hair, rode the swell of her belly and ended in Clive, kneeling with reverent silence, his tongue worshipping at Nell's generous cunt.

When the crack of light from the open door had fallen across them, Emilia had stood stony for one long minute on the threshold, then clicked the door shut with a customary neatness, before gathering her gloves, her coat, from the foyer and making towards Bayswater. As she passed that side of the building she couldn't help herself glancing up towards Nell's office, but everything was still in darkness.

All night the image had returned to her, and now, as she glanced down at the immaculate package in her gloved hand, it superimposed itself on silver ribbon and paper scored to fold at right angles.

When she had first heard, on the office grapevine, that Nell was pregnant, Emilia's joy had been unbounded. And when Clive had asked her, between meetings, 'Any gossip, then?' she had inclined her head slightly with that preparatory pause and told him about it with a proprietary pleasure, made sincere through layers and layers of practice over the years of being a personal assistant. Clive left his half-drunk coffee on the edge of her desk, lifting the office cat out of his path before bouncing off to meet with the printer.

'There'll be a collection, of course?'

She nodded slightly.

'Here. Take this fiver to start it off.'

She bent and slid a fresh buff envelope out of her stationery drawer, and held it beneath her downturned palms, feeling through the thin paper all the new paths, new possibilities that were already opening up. Slowly she slid in the five-pound note and added one to match it, shining with barely suppressed hope.

It had been much too early really, but doing it had made it all seem more real. She had gone down to Regent Street and spent a fruitless lunch hour sweeping the mother-and-baby departments, sorting briskly through possibilities and as briskly discarding them. She thought of the usual gifts – of what she might give to a friend, or to her several godchildren – and imagined the superior half-smile, the amused catch in the voice, if Nell were to unwrap a silver rattle, a tiny bracelet, or, God forbid, a Peter Rabbit breakfast set.

There seemed to be no room in the girl for sentimental considerations: the romance of motherhood apparently meant little or nothing to her. There were ways of behaving, and Nell fitted no known pattern. When Emilia had asked politely about her home arrangements, and whether she was getting on well with a nursery, there had again been that barely-concealed smile, then the emotionless recital of fact, as though she were communicating with a moron. Nell didn't feel it necessary to make a 'nest' for her child (the inverted commas hovered in the air between them, borne up by sarcasm) – she was just going to bed it down in her room in an old cot her aunt had passed on. When she herself had been a baby, her mother hadn't even found she needed that, but had used a drawer . . .

Not for one second did Emilia believe her. It was just another example of the inverted oneupmanship that Emilia had despised in Nell since the day she had interviewed her in Clive's office one lunchtime.

They were looking for a secretary to help some of the editors deal with their letters, perhaps to do a little proofreading if bright enough, and Nell, with her Oxbridge degree and her state education seemed useful, if not quite the right face for the job. Looking at Nell's endless CV, Emilia had tried to crack the ice: 'Well, you seem to be quite a bright girl, don't you?'

She had seen the younger woman's face harden ever so slightly, and realized with a certain sudden pleasure that she was feeling patronized. But Nell had kept her temper, and 'I think we may be able to offer you the job,' said Emilia, while at the same time her stomach was lifting and billowing with nerves. There seemed a sort of dark purpose in Nell – if Emilia had been fanciful, she might have called it the organized threads of evil – that filled Emilia with a sense of brooding chaos. To compensate, she had taken a deep breath, gained a little time, leant back in Clive's swivel chair and spun on the shiny surface of the desk his letter opener that was shaped like a miniature brass sword, so that it pointed first at Nell, then at herself, on and on. And while it spun, she talked about her years of publishing experience, until she could see she had cowed Nell into abandoning the hint of righteous rebellion that had been stirring in her eye. Nell was unsure of Emilia's status or power – probably thought she was an editor. It wasn't until beginning work the following week that Nell discovered Emilia was the managing editor's secretary. But by then she was well and truly under her thumb.

Liberty had yielded an exotic shawl in a soft fabric of twisted reds and yellows, edged in silver thread, and Emilia finally settled on it as being the sort of thing the office would want her to spend their money on. It was a gift that would have them imagining a nursing Nell who wore it while she cuddled her baby in a high-backed chair. But Emilia found it almost impossible to assemble the idea of Nell in maternal mode – although she could quite see that those hips would have no problem whatsoever in squeezing a little new life into the world.

God, by the look of her, the girl was born to be fecund! But it had taken her long enough.

At first she had worked for Emilia: typing, photocopy-ing, rushing to meet the needs of Emilia's periodic panics in the rush to keep Clive happy. For much of the week he was absent, and then he was back, demanding action and accomplishment. Emilia knew she was not really as terribly efficient as she seemed. When he was away she fell into a lassitude where she was constantly active and achieved next to nothing. As soon as Clive breezed in, she needed someone to help her make up lost ground. Nell would eye her knowingly, as she flitted purposelessly round her office, leaning insolently against the doorframe, her long hair swinging around her.

'I'll come back later, when you've got something you want me to do.'

The following week, she would lift some huge pile of photocopying out of Emilia's arms and do it quickly, without complaint, in half the time it would have taken Emilia.

Emilia's colleagues – the women with gold braid on their shoes, with whom she habitually shopped at lunchtime – watched with envy. 'You're lucky to have her,' they said, but Emilia kept her counsel.

'You'll lose her yet, though. That one's got ambition.'

It filled her with a quiet desperation that they should miss the just-hidden scorn that was directed at her.

More and more often, she found herself pausing: in the small, steamy bathroom of her Bayswater mansion flat; between drinks at a supper party with a few old friends; as the lights went down for the first act of some play. The image of Nell, laughing, cloaked in her own hair, would skate across her mind and leave her with a small bitterness whose after-effects the evening would never quite obliterate, although she often forgot the cause. Arriving at work began to seem a triumph over some minor ordeal; going home at the end of the day was more than pleasure.

Emilia found that she was counting on Nell's ambition to remove her altogether. Frequently she found her leafing surreptitiously through the *Guardian* jobs pages on a Monday, the paper spread haphazardly across her desk, half-hidden by the waterfall of her hair and the office cat. Even the cat seemed to love Nell, along with the rest of the office. Emilia wished it good riddance. She knew that *she* would never wear black velour to work when by six o'clock it was so thoroughly coated in the tiny white-rooted, ginger hairs. And the cat had always filled her with a sense of discomfort – a thrill of fear that she knew had something to do with the possibility that at any moment it could drop down dead. She ignored the *Guardian* reading and resolved that anything was worth it to have the girl finally gone.

One day, shortly after Nell had been moved full time into the copy-editing room by a perceptive personnel manager, Emilia came out of her office to find Nell sympathizing matily with her replacement over some procedural anomaly. The new secretary had been smiling up at her, while Nell's hair hung over the desk, hemming the two of them in like a cloud. 'The most dreadful system,' Nell had been saying.

Emilia watched the two of them together, and there was a turn to Nell's head that said how *egalitarian*, how *classless*, how *mature* she was. Instantly she was fired with a red and boiling rage that stunned her with its violence. Nell looked up, caught Emilia's eye and paused in mid-stream, then smiled.

'Just *which* dreadful system?' Emilia had demanded, struggling, and failing, she immediately realized, to keep the anger out of her voice. 'And what gives *you* the right to pontificate on it?' It was the smile that had driven her to it.

For a second, a slightly wounded expression crossed Nell's face, and then the insolence had returned to it, along with the smile. In the following days she had become even more distant from Emilia, even more outwardly polite, even more ambitious, and Emilia struggled not to enjoy the small ways in which she could make the other woman's life difficult. The pleasure was momentarily sweet, but it fed the nagging, raging visions that began to haunt the corners of her waking hours.

And the dead animals, too, came to haunt her.

Ever since Emilia had been a little girl, she had been terrified of dead animals. Anything live she could cope with, although she wasn't fond of cats, shied away from dogs, which seemed so rough, so unpredictable, so unclean. She could face down a spider and her brother had taught her to stroke the velvet nap of a bumblebee, but when life had departed and the body began to decay, she was filled with a screaming, revolted horror that was difficult to convey to others, and even more difficult to explain.

When life was particularly strained, she couldn't go into her dark garage at night without pushing a stick out in front of her, her arms stiff with fear in case it met with a soft solidity that could be a dead bird, but might be as bad as a cat. Once, motoring in Wales, she had seen a dead dog in the hedge, its fur flapping in the car's slipstream, and she had pressed her thin fingers across her mouth, choking down the words, hardly daring to turn to her companion and explain in case he should suggest they go back and do something with the body. After a couple of miles she could bear it no longer.

'Do you think we ought to go back?'

'Go back?' he had said. 'Why, whatever for? We'd be no use to it now, the poor beast. And do you really want some irate farmer breathing down our necks with a twelve-bore tucked under his arm?'

Relieved, she had sunk back into her seat and tried to put the image out of her mind.

But that night she dreamt she was crouching in the wet hedge, pressing the crumbly earth into two circles under her knees, staining the cream flannel of her skirt. The dog's stiff body stood before her, locked at the knees into a semblance of alertness, empty in the eyes. The strange intelligence that moves in animals had disappeared like smoke. The hand of order and archaic pattern that fans migrating birds, drives the cat to tease its prey, marshals insect colonies – the pattern that gives the eyes of a bird the same shy certainty as the eyes of a horse – was gone, and the emptiness that remained seemed only to underline the absence, the unnatural lack of something benign. Peering up into the sightless eyes, she edged her own nose up towards its rigid snout, inches from the cold meat that would warm with decay, and in that moment she knew that the cruelty of that removal was worse than any positive betrayal could have been. She felt alone in a godless world. There was nothing to rely on in that dead body – it was changing as she watched it. Who could guarantee that tomorrow everything would be where it should be: the eyes in their sockets; the paws on the ends of their legs? And all around her rose the stench of decaying dogflesh.

The next day she had faked up a phone call from the office. She asked her friend to take her home.

When Nell was promoted to manage the copyediting room, she had sometimes to draw on Emilia for help. She always did it with the utmost tact, careful never to indicate by word or gesture that the situation had once been reversed. Quite unfairly, Emilia recognized, she found this irritating. If only the girl would once lose her temper, her control, she felt they would be more equal. As it was, they continued to play the circling game, moving gingerly around each other – when Emilia stabbed out, Nell would find a way to elude her, pushing her away with the stillness of her emotionless eyes.

Occasionally, Emilia tried to tell someone about it, but it was hard to find someone who would bitch with her. There was always too long a pause, one too many blinks, as the confidante felt around for a reasoned answer to what seemed to them so eminently unreasonable. Emilia was terrified they would think her jealous. In the end she abandoned any effort to express the peculiar tensions of the situation. Instead, she watched Nell watching her, and began, between visions of retribution, to feel slightly afraid. But her fear only really began to gnaw at her after she knew she had been seen outside the game butcher's.

It was a bright, hot day in October, the thick dust of summer drifting slightly in the breeze that showed it should have been autumn. Emilia had lunched at Fenwick's with a few friends, and she had a couple of pairs of sale shoes tucked under her arm in a green-and-white plastic bag, when she turned out of Carlos Place, waiting to cross on to Mount Street. She didn't usually return to the office that way, but made her way back by the quieter, more residential streets. Now, heavy with heat and lunch, she stood absently on the island in the middle of the road, eyeing the taxis bowling past, waiting for a break in the traffic.

And then a flash that looked like fur streaked across towards her, narrowly missing the wheels of a cab that pulled up sharply to avoid it. Horrified but mesmerized, Emilia turned to stare after it, then swung back to the cruel wheels that had nearly crushed out the smoke at her feet. A sickness rose in her throat, and she stepped out into the road, trying to cross, to get away, before the taxi could restart its stalled engine. She reached the kerb in a couple of uneven jumps, but continued to stare back, her neck swivelling first to the pavement where it stretched in front of her, then up towards Grosvenor Square, where some animal had long since thoroughly vanished. Her breathing was ragged in her chest as she half-walked, half-ran, backwards up the street, the thump of her feet a counterpoint to the thump in her chest. Half her mind told her that people were staring at her, and then Nell was beside her, laughing, her mouth in happy shapes, saying, 'Oh, you'd better look out, Emilia. You'd better watch your step.'

With one breath she prepared to let rip her anger, her sarcastic wit. Then she felt the tangling in her hair, turned, and with the next breath she screamed.

There had been a reason she didn't use Mount Street, and she had just remembered it.

The game butcher's was festooned with strings of dead birds, slightly bloody, their feathers a little dulled; with stiff rabbits, hanging down like dead babies. And in the window more dead animals of uncertain age had been grotesquely resurrected, to strut with glass eyes, their insides held together with kapok and formaldehyde, advertising the appeal of their decaying brethren.

It was Nell who picked up the shoes where they had scattered in the gutter, but by that time Emilia had gone. Someone found her in the ladies' cloakroom, scrubbing frantically at her hair in a basin of scalding water. She could not look at Nell for a week without trembling with anger and fear, and when she finally calmed down, she knew that she must speak to Clive. These things had gone on long enough.

Clive was strangely immovable. He circled her where she sat at her desk, and sucked his teeth, and said, 'Oh *come on*, Emilia,' in a kind way, as though there were some debate about the truth of what she had to say.

'But now *she knows*,' said Emilia, over and over, spinning the letter opener on the desk with an efficiency driven by her body, beyond the control of her mind. But Clive could not get out of her what it was that Nell now knew.

Eventually, he took her by the shoulders, held her with his eyes and spoke to her quietly about priorities and a happy working atmosphere and the three weeks of holiday that were owed her from the previous year. Emilia went off to walk the Welsh coast, to channel down into her legs and out across Cardigan Bay the restless energy that had driven the pointer. And when she returned, relaxed and windblown, it was to hear that Nell was pregnant.

All the office loved a pregnancy. It was a comfortable place, reasonably relaxed, and most people got on with each other, but the prospect of a new baby, growing in their regimented midst, intrigued them just because it was so alien. It promised light relief: the chance to talk about Pampers instead of print runs; of booties instead of indices. Nell, more than ever, thrived on the good wishes and attention. The women envied her and the men admired her, and nobody really asked about the baby's father. They knew vaguely that Nell had been married, but the husband to whom she'd been attached when she first began working with them was a shadowy figure in most people's imaginations, eclipsed by the vitality of the very present Nell. A few people knew of her divorce, but somehow the impact of the birth needed no questions about paternity. It was as though everyone accepted that Nell might have a baby by herself if she so chose. A few people muttered about sperm banks and one-night stands, but nobody really probed.

Only Emilia wondered at the sudden blossoming of maternity in one so very unmaternal. She wondered at night, when she woke suddenly out of nothingness, and she wondered during the day, as through the reinforced glass of her office door she watched Nell circling from room to room, collecting a manuscript from one desk, picking up questions and a few compliments at another, dropping off gossip at a third. Eventually she could stand it no longer. She waited until she felt confident she had the words, then she called Nell in to see her on the pretext of discussing a stationery order.

'Did you want me?'

And there she was, smiling in the doorway, her stomach swelling under the flowered skirt, her hair swinging around her waist, each hand grasping the opposite wrist – slightly nervous, perhaps? – the cat at her feet.

'Draw up a chair, Nell, and tell me first of all how you're feeling.' Emilia's smile was careful, magnanimous, even benign.

'I want to know all about the joys of pregnancy, but first, do put out the cat, will you? And tell me how your ex-husband is, and what he thinks about the impending arrival.'

'Such a lot of questions,' smiled Nell, and half an hour later she bowed out of the office backwards, leaving Emilia little wiser, bound in by straight looks and polite answers.

The next morning Emilia came into her office to find a dead sparrow spreadeagled across the smooth grain of her desk. One of the cleaners remembered leaving the window open the night before, and the general consensus was that the poor thing must just have battered itself to death trying to find a way out. The walls were covered in small clumps of matted feathers. After a couple of hours and a handful of Valium Emilia was calm enough to go home in a taxi.

For nearly a week she paced the flat, seeing half-flattened hamsters in the kitchen linoleum, severed monkey heads in the wools of her sewing basket, desiccated stick insects between the panes of the double glazing. And superimposed on the whole corrupt menagerie was the round smile, the round stomach of Nell, swelling with superior knowledge and the incremental growth of a new creature. Even as Emilia thought about it there were eyes forming in the darkness of that woman's womb, coalescing out of the stinking humus, to take on the look from their mother. Oh, they were waxing now, but like everything else, they would wane, the sharp iris glitter dulling first behind the milky cataracts of old age, then running back into the crumbly earth. It made her sick – literally – and she shut her eyes tight against the foul mess she hawked up into her basin every time she let the rage take hold of her belly and shake it like a rag doll.

'But if she's having a baby, she'll be about to leave,' her brother reminded her, ringing from Australia, where he had settled with his family.

Emilia remembered the present she was to buy, and immediately her stomach felt more settled. She promised herself she would go down to Regent Street the next day. Back at work nice and early, then a long lunch hour, browsing with purpose. She steeped a lime blossom teabag in hot water, ate a couple of water biscuits and told herself she felt much better. And already she did.

She walked in the next day, trying to establish some firmness in her legs. Met the night security guard, still on the desk.

'Morning, miss.' Everything as normal. Took the lift to the seventh floor, and the receptionist asked her how she felt. She felt fine, she told her, and then up the corridor most of the offices were still and empty. But from twenty feet away she could see a black velour back filling her doorway, and Clive had his hand on the shoulder, picking off tiny hairs, smiling, laughing.

'You and that cat Alice,' he was saying, and holding up the tiny, white-rooted ginger hairs to the light.

'Of course, you know what these are?' More joint laughter.

'You are covered in *small pieces* of Alice . . .' And then he had seen Emilia half-way down the corridor and hastily removed his hand. Nell turned, and Emilia saw from her face that she was ever so slightly shaken, surprised. They drew apart.

'Much better, I hope, Emilia?'

His face dared her to challenge the normality of it all. It was that which finally convinced her. She stared fixedly at Nell's stomach, and then, '*Much* better, thank you,' she said, and sidled past them to slip in behind her desk. She rearranged her pencil tray, feeling them watching her together, and then Clive sighed heavily, and when she looked up the doorway was empty.

At eleven o'clock the personnel manager rang her to say how delighted they all were that Nell had decided to return to work after her maternity leave. It was at seven-thirty that she witnessed Nell, spreadeagled across her desk, in three-way communion with her baby and its father.

She took the shawl home and wrapped it, but she knew now that it should be she who unwrapped it, teasing it from its plastic bag, its perfectly-scored paper, extracting it with the greatest care from the tissue paper breathing softly around the silk. No nursing shawl this, but the finest of shrouds. And, as she pressed the tiny, pliable parcel between her cool palms, she already felt what it would be like to face down death in order to live. She already knew how the tiny, satiny limbs would feel as she wrenched them from their sockets like chicken bones. How the brass sword would feel in her fingers as she pointed towards murder through the ginger, white-rooted fur. And how she would shout in God's face, whether or not he showed it to her, as she drained it away through the force of her own hands, then wrapped the framework to give to his handmaid. A present: the life and death of her familiar. Her destiny, spreadeagled on a desk.

The fertilizer man

Mark Morris

Mark Morris was born in June 1963 in Bolsover. He graduated in 1984 and lives with his wife, the artist Nel Whatmore, in Leeds. In 1988, after three years on the dole, he became a full-time writer on the enterprise allowance scheme. Within six weeks a novel, Toady, which had taken him two and a half years to write was accepted by Piatkus. His second, Stitch, appeared in 1991. His short stories have sold to Fear, Me, Dark Dreams, The Dark Side, Dark Voices 3, Skeleton Crew, Final Shadows and Narrow Houses.

Among his interests he includes 'seeing friends off at midnight on long, potentially lethal journeys, and breaking other people's ornaments'. His main ambition, outside of writing, is to see Leeds United win the first division championship.

Clearly, it would be unwise to give up the writing career.

He creates threatening atmospheres with either supernatural forces or malign characters driving one set piece into the next. His new novel – The Immaculate – and the paperback of Stitch are due in 1992. 'In a way, The Immaculate was written as a reaction to Stitch. I think of my first three novels in terms of colour. Toady is multi-coloured, a phantasmagorical explosion, whereas Stitch is a black book, very dark and brooding. The Immaculate is white – it relies for its power on atmosphere and suggestion, and is the antithesis to Stitch's explicit probings into sin and sexuality. The themes of The Immaculate are positive – reunion, redemption and love. I see the three novels almost in terms of a trilogy which showcase the themes, moods and styles I will be adopting in future work.'

The fertilizer man

Tosho leaned back on his spade and looked out over his allotment with satisfaction, his old back throbbing with a steady pain. Two hours ago the allotment had been a weed-clogged patch of tired, grey earth, but now the soil was rich, dark, moist – perfect for vegetables. He swept off his cap and wiped his forehead with a grimy sleeve, his face red and shiny. Digging over the allotment had been a slog, especially for a man his age, but Tosho didn't mind. He came from a family to whom the work ethic was as important as mother's milk.

He looked up, past the allotments, past the council estate, to the squared-off peaks of the tower blocks beyond. That was the trouble with young people today, he thought; no moral fibre. Too many of them sat in offices, typing out reports that no one ever read, breathing air out of packets. He shook his head sadly. That wasn't the way to live, was it? God didn't create the land so that people could rot their lives away in office blocks.

He pulled open his shed door, making a mental note to oil the creaking hinges, and placed his muddy spade carefully on a sheet of newspaper in the corner. He stretched his stubby limbs, clenched and unclenched his meaty hands. His body had been locked into a digging position and he groaned as he straightened up, spine crackling.

The sound of approaching voices caused him to look out of his shed window. A group of teenagers, six or seven of them, were clambering over the gate that led into the allotments. They were looking furtively around, sniggering, putting their fingers to their lips. Their leader was tall and wore a leather jacket. He had sharp, nipped features as though someone had taken a long piece of white plasticine, pinched out a nose, and made the eyes and mouth with three strokes of a needle. A greasy quiff flopped over his forehead. He said something to the others and they laughed obediently. He led them to a greenhouse, said something else, and pointed at the ground. Immediately two of the boys stooped and began to pull small half-grown carrots from the earth. The thin boy went into the greenhouse where Tosho could see him through the glass, stuffing his jackets with tomatoes, jerking them off their plants with easy, languid movements, all the time his weasel-like face holding an arrogant leer.

Tosho felt a black wave of rage engulfing him. His chest constricted into bitter knots, his temples throbbed with anger. He snatched up his spade and yanked open the door.

'What the bloody hell do you think you're up to?' he bellowed. He clenched the spade firmly in both hands and lumbered towards them.

Heads snapped up. The two boys who had been stealing carrots dropped their loads and bolted away like startled rabbits.

'Come back here, you little buggers!' Tosho shouted, but at the sound of his voice, the boys simply increased speed, leapt over the wooden gate with a fear-spurred agility, and disappeared up the road. Angrily Tosho turned his attention to the other boys clustered around the greenhouse. One of them was shouting into the greenhouse whilst the others stood, fidgeting nervously, not daring to leave without their leader.

'I'll have you, you buggers!' yelled Tosho, picking

his way carefully between the even rows of vegetables. The tall, thin boy with the weaselly face emerged from the greenhouse, laden down with tomatoes. He looked unconcernedly in Tosho's direction, then began to stroll nonchalantly towards the gate, the other boys falling into step behind him. They tried to imitate their leader's arrogant swagger, but were given away by their jerky movements and occasional backward glances. Tosho was still some way off and knew he could not catch them before they reached the gate, so, frustrated, he resorted to the next best thing – verbal threats.

'You just come back here, you bloody hooligans! I'll tan your bloody hides for you!'

The thin boy stopped, turned slowly, and regarded Tosho through slitty eyes. Apart from his perpetual leer his face revealed nothing. Then he mockingly raised a hand and jabbed a two-fingered gesture in Tosho's direction. 'Piss off, you senile old bastard!' he called in a thin, whining voice. His words were met with a stringy burst of nervous laughter from the other boys. They crowded round their leader like baby chicks round a mother hen, watching Tosho warily. After a moment the thin boy jerked his head and they began to stroll away.

Tosho, watching them, was speechless with rage. His face and neck flushed a livid red, and for a moment he was so angry that he couldn't move. Then a strangled cry erupted from his vocal cords, he waved the spade in an arc above his head, and he charged, his anger making him oblivious to what lay beneath his feet.

The boys scattered for the gate, leaving a trail of tomatoes and carrots behind them. One by one they vaulted over it, stopping briefly on the other side to jeer at their pursuer before disappearing out of sight round the corner of the road.

Tosho thumped to a stop like a huge clockwork caveman. His anger seethed and bubbled impotently. His heart was thumping much too quickly, causing a biting pain in his chest. He suddenly felt very weary and the spade in his hands seemed to have become much heavier. He stared at the spot where the boys had disappeared, but found it difficult to focus. Unpleasant cactus shapes blinked behind his eyelids in a red and green swarm.

'Are you all right, sir?'

The voice startled Tosho and he whirled round. A tall man in his thirties, wearing an immaculate business suit, was standing directly behind him. The man had chiselled, tanned features, beautifully groomed hair and perfectly polished shoes. A slim briefcase was tucked neatly under his arm. Tosho gaped stupidly at him for a moment, mouth opening and closing like a worried goldfish. Where had the man come from? The allotments covered a large, flat area and there was absolutely no way he could have crept up without Tosho knowing about it. It was as though he had suddenly popped up from the ground like a subterranean jack-in-the-box.

One of the man's perfectly shaped eyebrows rose a little. He had a friendly, yet strangely immobile face. 'Are you quite all right?' he repeated.

'Yes . . . yes . . . I, er . . . just those bloody kids,' mumbled Tosho. His body drooped as the rage ebbed from him.

'I saw the whole thing. Perfectly dreadful,' said the man. He stretched out a supporting hand to steady Tosho's swaying body. His grip closed like a clamp around Tosho's forearm and he steered him effortlessly back to the shed. Once there, he went inside and reappeared with a wooden box which he set down on the ground. Tosho thanked him and sank onto it gratefully.

'Do you know who those boys were?' asked the man.

'Yes . . . that is, I've seen them around. They're always in bother. Just a bunch of bloody troublemakers.' Tosho looked up as a thought struck him. 'You aren't from the police, are you?'

The man smiled and shook his head. 'I'm afraid not, sir,' he replied in his deep, melodious tones. 'I am a salesman.'

'A salesman?' echoed Tosho, baffled. He looked at the man's shoes. He found it faintly disturbing that not a trace of mud was present on either. 'Indeed, sir,' replied the man, flashing a professional smile. His teeth were pure white and very straight.

'But . . . but what do you sell?' Tosho enquired. It struck him that he wasn't particularly interested, but something about the man's manner had compelled him to ask the question. The man leaned a little closer and his smile widened. Tosho recoiled slightly. He felt uncomfortable, and decided it was because of the man's eyes: they were very dark, almost black, and they were scrutinising him with a hypnotic, unblinking steadiness.

'Let me show you an example,' said the man. He opened his briefcase, took out a white cardboard packet and handed it to Tosho. Tosho took it automatically and began to read the lettering on the front: *Gro-fast Fertilizer – Amazing Results Guaranteed*. The rest of the lettering was too small for Tosho to make out without his glasses. He looked up, bewildered.

'Fertilizer?' he said. The fertilizer salesmen Tosho had previously encountered had all been thick-set farmers with straw hats and trousers stiff with pigshit.

'And a variety of other agricultural products,' replied the man smoothly. 'But this is our latest item. It is a specially formulated concentration of elements guaranteed to enrich the soil and produce the healthiest vegetables possible.'

Tosho frowned, suspicious. The man's wide smile was beginning to irritate him. 'How come I've never seen none of this in the shops?' he asked, matching the man's steady gaze with an accusatory one of his own. The man's face never altered.

'Usually we deal in bulk orders,' he explained, 'but this fertilizer is still in something of an experimental stage. We therefore decided to start by giving free samples to a number of accommodating landowners. To judge its progress and effectiveness, as it were.'

A small bell tinkled happily in Tosho's mind at the magic words 'free samples', and his red face crinkled into a friendly beam.

'I'll tell you what, mister,' he began in a manner that suggested he was doing the other a great favour, 'I'll take one of them free samples and put it on me own allotment. I don't mind doing some of your experimenting for you.'

The man nodded graciously. 'Thank you, sir,' he replied humbly, 'that would be most kind.'

'Wait on, though,' said Tosho as a possible loophole occurred to him, 'what if this stuff ruins me crop? I'll want compensation.'

'Absolutely no problem, sir. In such an eventuality you would receive the highest market value for all produce spoiled. Here is a number on which I can be contacted.' The man reached into the inside pocket of his jacket and handed Tosho a small card. It simply read *Gro-fast Products – 444555*. 'If you have any complaints whatsoever, don't hesitate to call.'

Tosho took the card with a soily thumb and forefinger, glanced briefly at it, and stuffed it into the pocket of his worn, ill-fitting jacket. 'Well, thank you very much. Very kind, I'm sure,' he said.

'Not at all, sir,' replied the man smoothly. He looked up at the sky as though gauging the time by the sun, then said, 'Well, I must be going, though I shall call by again presently. Goodbye.' He extended a brown hand with elegantly manicured fingernails. Tosho shook it tentatively. The man's hand was pleasantly warm and his grip was firm. With a final smile he turned and strode away.

Tosho watched him until he disappeared behind a hedge, and then examined the box of fertilizer the man had given him. He tore off the corner of the cardboard top and upended the box into his palm. A fine reddish powder trickled out. Tosho sifted it with his forefinger, then held it up to his nose and sniffed. Funny-looking stuff, he thought; almost like flour, but red instead of white. He fetched his spectacles from the shed and read the instructions carefully: *Plant vegetables as normal, then sprinkle liberally with Gro-fast fertilizer. Allow time for fertilizer to absorb into soil before watering.* Tosho was a little disappointed. Was that all? Despite the fact that the box had been a gift, he couldn't help feeling somehow cheated.

He spent the rest of the day planting seeds in his newly dug garden. His mouth watered as he thought of the potatoes, carrots, peas, cabbages, radishes, onions and other vegetables he would be bringing home in the following months. Vegetables always tasted much better when you grew them yourself, he always said, and this year looked as though it was going to be particularly good.

When the seeds had been planted, Tosho used the new fertilizer on them. He ripped open the packet fully and sprinkled the red dust over the earth with a heavy hand. It lay on the soil like a blanket of blood, and then as Tosho watched it seemed to mingle with the earth and become absorbed into it; actually seemed to become one with the soil. He was amazed. He had never seen anything like it! The fertilizer seemed to enrich and nourish the soil, gave it a healthy red sheen that caused it to stand out amongst the neighbouring plots of earth, even the most carefully tended of which looked dull and sterile by comparison. Tosho was well pleased. If the stuff worked as well on vegetables as it did on the soil, he was in with a chance of making a clean sweep of the prizes in the vegetable section of that year's local Horticultural Society Show.

He whistled with the joy of a highly satisfied man as he pushed his old wheelbarrow into the shed at the end of the day. He was always reluctant to leave his allotment, but it was getting dark and he didn't want to be late for his supper. Besides, he was looking forward to boasting about his new wonder fertilizer to his mates in the local that evening. He locked the shed door and set off home, still whistling. By now, the distressing episode with the boys that morning had slipped completely from his mind.

* * *

Mark Morris

Colin Deakin remembered, though. He was not too clever when it came to remembering historical dates or mathematical equations, but those people who had crossed him were meticulously filed away in his mind under the heading 'Hit List', and Tosho was one of those people. It was Tosho's fault that Deakin had not bought the motorbike that afternoon. It was Tosho's fault that that smarmy git in the showroom had sold it to someone else.

Deakin had needed those tomatoes: all of them. He had planned to nick enough vegetables from the allotments to raise a tenner down at the market. That was all he'd needed for the bike. Ten more fucking lousy quid. But now, because of that stupid, interfering old bastard, he'd lost the chance to buy the machine he'd had his eye on for weeks.

Deakin wouldn't stand for that; he'd show that old shit. He got out of bed and quietly opened a drawer. Everyone was asleep by now and he didn't want to wake them. He took a black t-shirt, black jeans, black boots and black gloves from the drawer and pulled them over his pasty frame. He slicked his hair back out of habit with a few practised flicks of his oily comb and zipped up his leather jacket. Silent as sleep he went downstairs, furtively unlocked the front door, and crept out into the night. He headed towards the allotments, keeping to the darkest corners, sliding from wall to wall like a leather-clad eel. Finally he reached the gate over which he and his mates had jumped that morning.

His cruel, pinched features surveyed the surrounding landscape. Satisfied that no one was around, he climbed nimbly over the gate. There were no streetlamps here, and it took Deakin a moment for his eyes to become accustomed to the gloom, though fortunately the moon provided an ice-cold light. Other moons slithered over the greenhouses, pools of white seemingly trapped within the glass.

Deakin crept cautiously over the uneven ground. Here

58

and there were small fences, little more than twine stretched between stakes hammered into the ground. In the half-light they were difficult to see, and Deakin had to move slowly to avoid tripping over them. Tosho's allotment lay over the far side, and the teenager cursed the old man every muddy inch of the way.

He was within thirty yards of the allotment when he suddenly stopped. Had he heard something? He strained his ears to listen, but all he could hear was the faint sound of a car receding into the distance somewhere. He was about to continue forward when he heard it again – the bump and thud of clumsy movement from somewhere in front of him.

Deakin dropped to his knees and became perfectly still, merging with the darkness. Squinting ahead, he thought he could see a dim shape moving around near the old man's shed. Surely the old git wasn't senile enough to stay here until this late at night? Deakin peeled back his sleeve and looked at the watch he had stolen from Woolworth's: 12.23. He shuffled on all fours to a nearby hedge so that his black silhouette would not be seen against the silvery glow of the sky, and stood up slowly. He peered through the gloom towards Tosho's shed.

There *was* something moving about down there: it seemed to be scuffling around with weird, jerky movements. But all Deakin could make of it was a vague white shape, like someone crawling on all fours.

He was intrigued, and a little scared, though he would not have admitted that to anyone. He crept closer, his body feeling as though it had seized into a taut knot of muscle, making his movements stiff and unnatural. He clenched his fists tightly and tried to blot out his unease. He saw the vague white shape bobbing through the air and round the side of the shed, out of sight. Somehow, not being able to see the shape made Deakin feel worse, not better.

He noticed a rake with a broken handle leaning against a wooden box and snatched it up. Immediately a feeling of security swept over him. He always felt strong and powerful with a weapon to hide behind. He picked his way over to the shed and tiptoed stealthily around its side, raising the rake slowly like an executioner. His jawbone was clenching and unclenching in an effort to keep the saliva from drying in his mouth. Though he was scared, he was also angry. What was frightening about a white blob that moved in the darkness? he thought, and the answer came: nothing; nothing at all. Yet despite his logic the fear was there, like an anvil in his chest, and it wouldn't go away.

There was nothing round the side of the shed. Nothing, that is, except ground and weeds and the shed wall, all cut into harsh black and white tones by the cast of the moon. Deakin realised he had been holding his breath and exhaled slowly. The uneven ground, dotted here and there with the occasional greenhouse or garden shed, stretched silently to the tall hedge which bordered the allotments. There were no white shapes bobbing in the darkness, and there were no thuds of movement either. Deakin smiled, stepped forward – and his foot plunged into empty space. As he began to fall, he instinctively jammed the end of the rake into the earth to steady himself, but his ankle twisted and he crashed to the ground.

He lay for a moment, panting, his body jarred by the fall and his right foot dangling in space. His thoughts were wild and illogical. It was as though someone had snatched away a plug of reality from beneath his foot, leaving a rent full of nothingness. He pushed himself slowly upwards, wincing at the pain in his bruised ribs and ankle. He lifted his right foot gingerly out of the hole he had stepped into, stood up and brushed himself down. The hole was about three feet in diameter and seemed to tunnel under the shed wall. Deakin examined it curiously. It looked like a foxhole, or . . . or . . . it came to him suddenly. A badger's set! Was that what he had seen in the darkness – a badger? Deakin pushed the end of the rake into the hole to see how far down it went. The hole was deep, plunging about five feet before curving round under the shed wall. It must be a bloody big badger, Deakin thought. Why, he could probably crawl through that tunnel himself.

Curiosity was getting the better of him now. He decided to have a look in the shed, see how big the badger really was. He had never seen a badger before, but he had heard they were vicious bastards if cornered. Gripping the rake and steeling himself, Deakin kicked at the lock on the shed door.

It wasn't quite as ramshackle as it looked and his pinched features creased as the impact caused pain to spear up through his bad ankle. Furthermore, the noise that his boot made on the wood was amplified by the stillness of the night, so much so that Deakin was sure the vibrations could be felt throughout the neighbourhood. He stood for a moment and listened, but heard nothing. Satisfied that his attack on the door had gone undetected, he tried again. This time he hooked the end of the rake through the rusty padlock, stood round the corner of the shed, and heaved on the protruding end of the rake. Bit by bit the screws parted from the wood and eventually the entire lock came away with a tearing sound. The shed door swung open.

Deakin peered into the building, wrinkling his nose at the musty smell. Moonlight filtered through the grime on the tiny window, enabling him to make out a few vague shapes. There was a workbench along one wall, stacked with flowerpots, tools, and some bags of weedkiller. Larger tools such as rakes and spades hung on hooks on the opposite wall. Tucked in one corner was a wheelbarrow piled high with weeds. Although the shed was relatively small, the clutter provided ample room in which an animal could conceal itself. Deakin took a few cautious steps inside. He had a sudden uncomfortable feeling that eyes were watching him, sheltered in the blackness.

'Come out, you fucking rodent,' he hissed, jabbing savagely at a black bulky object in the darkness. His fear fed the flame of his anger. His voice rose. '*I fucking said come out!*'

He began to sweep the rake about like a practising

swordsman, prodding and slicing into every possible hiding place. It was unnerving that there were so many pockets of darkness in such a tiny area. Suddenly Deakin heard a minute sound, like something pressing itself back into the shadows, and he stopped dead, listening. The sound was coming from somewhere in front of him.

He extended the rake with excruciating slowness. His muscles felt bunched and cramped in his body as though gathering themselves for action. The rake-head touched something solid; something that gave a small grunt of surprise; *something that began to move!*

Deakin felt the rake suddenly wrenched from his hands. He staggered backwards, aware of a shape looming in the darkness, reaching for him. He plunged out of the shed doorway, grabbed the edge of the wooden door which was swinging gently on its hinges, and slammed it shut. He held it closed with one hand and looked desperately around for something to wedge it. After a moment he heard movement again from within, then a burrowing sound. Curiously he put his ear to the door, but just at that moment the burrowing stopped. Deakin held his breath – and heard the soft pad of footsteps behind him. He had forgotten about the hole. *Oh God, oh God.* His spit congealed like a golf ball as he turned to face whatever it was that had come out of the shed.

It was a man. *Just a man*, Deakin thought, *just a man.* But the man was naked, and even in this light Deakin could see that his body was perfectly smooth and hairless, and where his genitals should be there was only a small mound of smooth unbroken skin.

The teenager began to back away on rickety, spent legs. The man's handsome, regular features were fixed in an immobile grin, his teeth gleaming white, his hair, despite his crawl through the tunnel, beautifully groomed. In his hand he carried a spade.

Deakin turned and tried to run. His insides seemed to slacken and slosh in his body. His foot caught on something and he tripped and fell face-down into the mud, his gloved palms making a pitiful, hopeless smack as they hit the ground. He raised his head, his long face very white through the clumps of soil that clung to it. The man was stationary, hefting the spade in his hand.

Deakin's foot still rested on the half-buried log he had tripped over. With the intense horror of nightmare, he suddenly felt the log squirm beneath him. He looked down and his mouth opened in a soundless scream. It wasn't a log at all; it was a human arm, and it was breaking through the soil of the ground like some gruesome plant. Deakin's thin lips began to form a silent word, *No*, over and over again. He looked up desperately at the white orb of the moon and his face crumbled into tears.

The soil seethed beneath Deakin, and another arm began to break free from the earth. Before he could move, the hand on the arm flexed, then whipped forward and grabbed his ankle. Deakin began to scream and thrash about, but the hand simply tightened its grip.

Alerted by the struggle, the man with the spade jerked into motion again. Unhurriedly he strode towards Deakin's writhing form. Deakin's last sight before he blacked out was the man standing astride him, his perfect white teeth gleaming in the light of the moon.

Slowly, still smiling, the man raised the spade as though he was about to chop through something.

Which he did.

Very early the next morning, someone could be seen picking his way through the allotments: a tall man wearing an immaculate suit. He was the man Tosho had met just the day before; the fertilizer salesman.

Unhurriedly the fertilizer salesman made his way over to Tosho's shed, a vague smile on his handsome face. In his hand was a large trunk which he carried with effortless ease. He noted the broken padlock on the shed door and nodded in satisfaction. He opened the door and went inside.

Twelve heads turned as one. Twelve identical, handsome faces smiled at him. The fertilizer salesman set the trunk down on the shed floor and opened the lid.

Inside were twelve brand-new suits, just like his own.

The little boy's room

Kevin Mullins

Kevin Mullins was born in Chiswick in 1963, and tells it much better than I could: 'Grew up in Leamington Spa, famous because of Betjeman's poem, "Death in . . .". At junior school I was about as popular as a corpse at a wedding party, so I stayed away as much as possible. One teacher put in a report that I was a "Skilled Vampire Artist". Later, an English teacher expressed concern at the narrowness of my reading material (horror, sf). Dad, who is Irish, often tells me the story of how, as a child, he met his brother, a member of the Irish Free State Army, and was told by him to go home. When he arrived he found his family grieving over his brother's body. It seems he was killed by the IRA some time before my Dad spoke to him.

'Mum gave me my love of cinema and started me writing as well. When bored she writes poems for her own amusement. I came to Leeds to go to Trinity & All Saints' College, which is Catholic though I am an atheist. I studied Theology & Public Media and got a degree. Upon finishing college I had a period of unemployment during which I wrote a screenplay about lesbian vampires in a teacher-training college, which someone at Central TV liked the first third of (ie. the bit before the vampires). I did a small business course, and became Quality Assurance Officer at RP Drugs. This job involves examining so many bottles that I sometimes dream about them.

'I've written a few short stories but never had anything published until now. I want to carry on writing stories. I also have an idea for a novel. However, I think my real ambition has always been to write screenplays.'

Kevin Mullins also makes a good strong cup of tea and lives in a room piled to the ceiling with books and magazines. His filing system for manuscripts rests on the colour of the envelope. The trouble is it's always brown. The first unsolicited submissions I received for this anthology were from Kevin Mullins. I nearly accepted one. Eight months later he sent me a new story, The Little Boy's Room, *and I didn't hesitate for a moment.*

The little boy's room

Noises through the window.
Lots of men shouting.
Lamplight shining. Making shadows move.
Can't sleep. No way.

Door slams.
'Be quiet. He's asleep,' comes her whisper.
It doesn't work.
Here he comes. Up the stairs in big boots.
'I want to see David,' he says.
He speaks like there's syrup in his mouth.
The door opens. Light shines. He's just a shadow.
Getting bigger. Moving closer.
'David!' he says.
David can smell him. Can feel his heat.
'David, I love you.'
He bends over. The smell gets worse. Lamplight falls on
his face. It's the face of a scary clown and David won't look.
Heat on David's cheek, then staggering-back sounds.
David opens his eyes.
In the doorway stands a sad scary clown.

The sound of water falling. Rain?
David sees the dark stain on the clown's trousers. The
mini flood . . . and little droplets dripping.

David screams. The man cries.
'Dirty Man! Dirty Man! Dirty Daddy! I hate you!'

David stared down at the coffin. The rain had almost
stopped. The service was ending. Susan held his hand
and he felt like a child again. But not a happy one. His
mother shed silent tears near by. From David there were
no tears, just steaming raindrops he didn't brush away.
Eventually they all waded back to their cars.

David forced down sandwiches and avoided relatives for
the rest of the afternoon. Susan did an unusual amount of
washing up. People said how nice she seemed. He should
marry her before she got away.

David wanted to get away from them.

Evening came. Most people left. His mother took David
into the back bedroom.

'I want you to have something,' she told him flatly.

'We can get that sorted out later, Mum.'

David felt uncomfortable here in the centre of his
childhood world. His mother ignored him. She pulled
an old suitcase out from under the bed and rummaged
through it. David stared at the poorly hung wallpaper.
Faded footballers kicking phantom half-balls.

'Here it is.' Some emotion had come back to his
mother's voice. She held in her hand a cheaply framed
photograph. David tried to look interested.

'I didn't know if you'd come today,' she confided
without looking at him.

'That's stupid, Mum. I wouldn't leave you alone, not
now.'

'David, listen to me.' She held the photograph towards
him. David could see that it showed a four-year-old
dark-eyed healthy boy dressed in a nightshirt and smiling
happily.

'David, you never saw the rest of him. How he could
be. You just saw the drink.'

David took the photograph from her.

'This is him?' he asked, with some distaste slipping out. His mother nodded.

'It's not as if he hit you, David,' she snapped, her eyes welling up. David said nothing. But what he thought was, 'He didn't need to.'

Even so, he took the picture. Just to please her.

Driving home, Susan studied the little boy whilst David took his aggression out on the traffic.

'He looks so sweet,' she said, quietly.

'He didn't smell so sweet,' David spat out. They said little more to each other for the rest of the journey.

Back in the flat, having finished unpacking, David had an idea. He picked up the photograph off the coffee table and took it into the bathroom, together with a nail and hammer. As he began his task Susan came in from the bedroom to see what the noise was.

'What are you doing?' she asked sharply when she saw David hanging the photograph over the toilet. David stared back at her, a savage grin on her face.

'I'm making sure he never gets caught short again.'

Later in bed: a smoothing voice.

'You must be more upset than you think.'

But it was his failure that upset David more than anything else.

The next morning and back to work. Four months before, David had been head-hunted by Decarde Miller Packaging after successfully guiding his last company through to the Quality Assurance British Standard 5750. Now he was doing the same for D.M.P. with two days to prepare a progress report for the vice-chairman of the parent company.

He began the first of those two days with a blinding headache. Susan had dug him out some paracetamol before setting off for a couple of days with her parents and her son, Toby. After his father died she'd offered not to go but he'd said that was stupid. Now, with his head throbbing as he stared at his notes, he wished he had someone to go home to.

The tannoy screamed for him. He picked up the phone.

'Hello, David, Gerry here. Are we going to try and slip that stuff through or not?'

'For God's sake, Gerry,' David shouted down the line. 'What's the point in slipping it past the bloody unions if they don't do it once it's there?'

'I don't think there's any call for that, David,' said Gerry coldly. 'I think I'd be better off discussing the matter with Frank. Thank you.' He rang off. If David hadn't had a headache he'd have bashed his skull against the nearest wall. Instead he drowned himself in coffee.

Throughout the day he managed to alienate at least a couple more key people by snapping at them or failing to listen properly to what they had to say. All the time the headache throbbed unabated.

David arrived home, collapsed on the settee and fell immediately to sleep. He floated in dreams of dark seas and starkly lit faces.

The telephone rang and he jerked back to consciousness, kicking over the coffee table. As his eyes focused, a jumble of magazines spread out on the floor before him. Shaking his head clear he picked up the receiver.

It was Susan. They traded smalltalk for a while, said they loved each other and then David was alone again. It wasn't until then that he noticed his headache had gone.

Grateful for the respite David went into the bathroom to relieve himself. The picture of his father stared down upon him. David had trouble letting go. He considered taking the photograph down, maybe even just throwing it away. But he was damned if he was going to do that. He closed his eyes, the tension abated and the flow began.

*   *   *

The next day and David woke up feeling that he could smooth all the feathers he had ruffled the day before. And that was precisely what he proceeded to do. A little anti-union chat with Gerry, the incorporation of half-heard ideas from yesterday into his report with due credit. By lunchtime he felt he was pretty much ready for the vice-chairman's visit the following day. Despite this he didn't have much of an appetite. He dwelt over a bacon sandwich from the canteen like it was a five-course meal. Too much adrenalin, he decided.

The afternoon was spent on fine-tuning. At 2.30 David began his review of interim recommendations.

At 4.30 the telephone woke him up again! Drowsily he looked at his watch. He'd been asleep at his desk for nearly two hours. What was he doing to himself?

The phone continued to demand attention. Eventually, David answered it. Frank, the Managing Director, was on the line.

'What are you doing in there, David? Dozing off? I'm just ringing to make sure you're ready for tomorrow.' David said he was.

He took his report home and worked on the whiteboard graphics to go with the presentation. He knew to stop working when his drawing hand started shaking. He made a quick phone call to Susan, she was due back late tomorrow or early the next day, then had an early night.

David started the day of the presentation by throwing up. He felt his father's dark baby eyes mocking him as he rested his head on the toilet seat and breathed deeply. A spot of vomit on his jacket meant he had to change his suit. Gathering up his report and whiteboard materials he left the flat feeling apprehensive, maybe even fearful. This was nothing new in itself but he'd never actually been sick before.

The drive to work calmed him. He knew what he wanted to say and how to say it. He'd done it all before, for

Christ's sake. He'd never met the vice-chairman but he didn't have a reputation as a monster or anything like that. Relax and enjoy the applause at the end, he thought.

Upon arrival David plunged into a sea of best suits, nervous smiles and pedantic attempts at efficiency. It wasn't just him, then. Everyone was the same. The two union reps sat in the Personnel Officer's office yawning tensely and checking the shine on their shoes. David checked the shine on his too, and found it to be okay.

A cup of coffee later and it was time for the curtain to rise.

When he entered the conference room David saw that the vice-chairman and most of the other people to be present had already arrived and were seated.

After the last in a long line of handshake rituals David attached his whiteboard pad to the presentation easel and shifted his notes on the table. As the last person, Gerry, entered, David got the company secretary to distribute copies of his written report.

The smalltalk died away and all eyes were on him.

'Gentlemen, this, er,' he held up the written report, 'this is where we stand with our preparations for B.S.5750. Obviously you can read the report at your leisure but my job today is to give you the general thrust and pinpoint, er, areas where we still need to consider adjustments.' He turned to the first graphic and began.

Halfway through and David was doing fine. Yawning and coughing had been kept to a minimum amongst the dozen people present. They had laughed when they should, asked some good questions, though the vice-chairman himself had so far remained silent, and received some satisfactory answers. David stood by the easel, illustrating a point using the revised organisational chart.

'Okay. So let's look at the relationship between the Q.A. Department and the Inspectors. It's pretty much . . .' David faltered. He felt a sudden unexpected warmth around his groin. He put his free hand in his trouser pocket and felt dampness. His cheeks began to redden.

Suddenly everyone was staring at the area below his waist. At the darkening patch between his legs and the drops of yellow liquid dripping into the carpet.

Somebody sniggered. David, semi-dazed, thought it might be Gerry. Two other people joined in. David, paralysed, soaking wet and with his face burning up, heard someone whisper, 'Disgraceful,' realised it was the vice-chairman, and decided to pretend to collapse. He fell to the floor and lay sodden and full of self-loathing as the sniggering stopped and Frank moved across to check his pulse.

When the nightmare began to lose its momentum and David was sent home from the hospital in a taxi – no one wished to risk their upholstery by giving him a lift – the general consensus, medical and otherwise, was that he had had some kind of breakdown. His blood was checked for alcohol but no traces could be found, so that had to be the explanation. David himself expressed no opinion and quietly spurned all half-hearted offers to stay with him overnight in his flat.

On arrival home he slowly stripped off the company overalls which had been provided for him and headed for the bathroom. His father's picture hung there to greet him. All the emotion David had managed to keep in check throughout the long afternoon and evening burst out of him and he grabbed the photograph and smashed it to the floor. The glass and frame shattered, going in all directions.

The little dark-eyed boy stared up at him. His smile seemed to betray a trace of sadness. David picked up the photo, shredded it with his hands, then flushed it down the toilet.

'Fuck you, you drunken bastard,' he screamed down the pan as the water carried it away. Then, carefully avoiding the broken glass, he climbed into the shower and turned the water full on. His tears were washed away as fast as they fell.

Washed, dressed in a bathrobe and restored to some level of rationality, David dialled the number of Susan's parents.

'Hello, Susan,' he said flatly.

'Oh, David.' Her voice was shaking. 'I've been trying to contact you for hours. Toby's been run over. Some bastard drunk hit him.'

'What?' said David, his voice still emotionless. Everything seemed distanced from him.

'It happened when we were coming out of the park. The hospital thinks he's just got a broken leg but they're keeping him in overnight. I've just come back to get some things. Can you come over, David?'

'Not tonight, Susan.'

'Why not?' she asked tersely.

'I just can't make the journey. I'll be there first thing tomorrow.'

'Is there anything wrong? You sound strange.'

David managed a wry smile.

'I'll tell you tomorrow. Look after Toby.'

'All right. I'll have to go. See you tomorrow.' She hung up.

David let out a long breath and closed his eyes. He didn't know what had happened to him and he wished he could forget the whole day.

He sat up and looked around the room, trying to find something to restore his spirits . . . He was about to sort through his video collection when his gaze fell on the bottle of table wine which was the only alcohol kept in the house. David removed it from its home in the cabinet and placed it on the coffee table. He sat back on the settee and stared at the bottle until everything else was out of focus. Then, it, too, blurred as consciousness fell away.

When David woke up, the darkness was almost total. He stood up, kicked something which tinkled and fumbled for the light switch. The bulb blazed and David had to shield his eyes. Looking down he saw the wine bottle lying on the carpet. It was empty but there were no signs of spillage.

The bathroom door was open and David, still puzzled by the absence of wine, moved towards it to ease his aching bladder.

When he reached the doorway he stopped dead. In the darkness a small shadow stood in front of the toilet. David could hear the trickling of water coming from its direction. Almost against his will he turned on the light.

A child in a clean white nightshirt stood with his back to David. There were damp patches on the tiles where the child had been walking in the room. It made no sound. There was no sound, but for David's heavy breathing.

As the child began to turn, David knew what he would see. He recognised the dark hair even before the innocence of the eyes and face were visible.

It was only when the boy smiled, revealing brown corpse-like teeth, and whispered oh so softly . . .

'David, I love you'

. . . that David surrendered control of his bladder for the second time that day. But this time he hardly noticed.

As the boy walked towards him he knew there were wetter things to come.

The rolling road to Kensal Green

Alan David Price

Alan David Price was born in Liverpool in 1949. Throughout his teens and 20s he produced a short (unpublished) novel, a children's story (serialised on radio) and a large quantity of poetry, published in little magazines, broadcast on radio and presented at readings. In the late 70s he turned to fiction again and has now written 30 stories, two of which – The House of the Broken Pediment *and* My Elongated Scar *– were broadcast on Radio 3. A Box of Swan – a film written for BBC2 – was broadcast in October 1990, and in 1991 a new script was commissioned by the First Film Foundation.*

Alan David Price lives in north London, 'where writing is combined with social work with children, and reflexology. Many interests, but especially watching too much world cinema, reading, listening carefully to Mozart, observing politics, travelling and keeping fit.' To be more precise about the location, he lives at Swiss Cottage, a short jog from Kensal Green Cemetery, the first of seven big cemeteries constructed around London in the early nineteenth century, when overcrowding in the parish graveyards presented an unpleasant and unhealthy problem.

With the Cold War over, the premise of The Rolling Road to Kensal Green *may seem outdated, until you reflect that thirty-six countries now operate or are planning to start up a nuclear power programme. You never know where the end of the world will be coming from next.*

The rolling road to Kensal Green

When I heard that there was still an hour left, I decided to run to Kensal Green cemetery. Should I lie expectant by the podium of Gruner's quattrocento sarcophagus? Forever looking skywards with the remains of Princess Sophia. Or humbly shelter in the facing Anglican chapel?

In dreams, I've imagined a rain of warheads on Kensal's Doric temple. That rear end of the cemetery by the canal and gasworks. Then the rain spreading to take in its inhabitants. Monolithic tombs, mausoleums, family vaults and the occasional wooden cross of a pauper. In seconds everything joining the great crater.

> And see undrugged in evening light the decent inn
> of death
> For there in goodness yet to hear and fine things to
> be seen.
> Before we go to paradise by way of Kensal Green

Poor G. K. Chesterton. Our rolling English road had led to this. Even my run wouldn't roll. From Kilburn High Road to Brondesbury Road. Queen's Park to Harvist Road. Then Kensal itself. The running would be fiercely straight. Save for a final, sharp turn to the right.

Oh Christ, the cat's gone and pissed on my tracksuit! Well, at least I can still smell what stains me. It's almost comforting. Like smelling this room, the sweat on my fingers, the musty pages of Chesterton's poetry. Afterwards someone (or something) might sniff my remains. Perhaps I'll have a special, fallout odour.

I'd like to think I'd retain my individual stink.

When you said you loved me did you mean it?
   Of course I didn't.
   Oh that's all right then. I've got the children in the car. The Hebrides?
   Yes the motorways will be full. Probably sealed off in places. But I'll make it. So long as the heather doesn't burn!

I wonder if the priest from Hampstead will be there? A little, squat man. His ankles perched on the tomb of William Mulready.

'This mediocre R. A. painter has a beautiful tomb. But Isambard Kingdom Brunel! Just another name on a plain, family headstone. Then again Thomas Hood and Thackeray have simple affairs. Generally bankers, statesmen and soldiers went for spectacular memorials. They gave the world blood and sacrifice. And we were not allowed to forget they ruled.'

In fifty-five minutes, a handful of rulers would survive.

Any similarity between them and long-dead authority would be erased. Their vested power hideously slighter. Ruling a closing nightmare for the sheltered few. Instead of a dream of progress for the bunkered masses.

Where's my glass? Cheap, cracked Japanese tumbler. Mary had no taste for choosing glassware! Whisky's still good though!

I wonder if the neighbours have whitewashed their windows? David won't have. Has a flat upstairs. Last night I heard him exercising against the floor. He'd sooner take an overdose than have his physique on fire. The narcissistic protection of a strong body. We said goodbye. Embraced. A different hugging to the one for my family. *Why don't*

you stick with them! screamed friends. What was the point?
The day I decided to leave my nuclear family I received
news that they were soon fully to be one.

The cemetery gates will be closed. Guard dogs installed.
A last, neat tidying up. Put the rubbish out and lock the
till. Shops where people cashed up for the last time (forget
extra change from the bank for the weekend). Offices
where typewriters were dutifully covered. I wonder if my
mother did her breakfast dishes? A lot went berserk. They
abandoned everything, killed one another, looted houses
and set fire to looted shops. It contradicted the orderly
calm that the protection booklet stressed. I once worked
for the Civil Service. Three years as a clerical officer.
The early eighties. I remember that sadly creased, pink-
coloured bus advertisement. Recruiting anyone with two
O levels for clerical jobs with the Ministry of Defence.

Patrick said he'd take a stomach pump along with a
bottle of Southern Comfort. Lie face up in the shopping precinct fountain. If the missiles failed to deliver,
he'd drag himself out. Take the pump and discharge his
bleary inside.

Everyone's leavetaking will be different. My wife will
just quietly sit on the bed. Continuing to meditate with
our frightened children pinned to the duvet. Whilst the
old man at the end of the street has sworn to crack his skull
against the wall of the betting office. Ladbroke's wouldn't
accept the ultimate bet. And I'm swiftly running into the
past (so neglected in the present) to the remembrance zone
of Kensal Green.

Celestine Salome Fergus – a beautiful name, a lovely
black woman. On the headstone (behind a transpar-
ent glass cover) lies your colour photograph. A blown-
up, passport shot. A shame the car accident reduced
you to that . . . uggh! I really ought to have disin-
fected this tracksuit! Already near the end of Canterbury
Road. Jogging! Hate that term! I'm running for a little
grace!

Quite warm today. Save another drink till Kilburn Lane.

Probably collapse when I get there. Swoon at the lion's feet of the family vault of Edmund Pickering. A banker who lived in Maida Vale. He possessed a pet lion. A crowned lion melting on a ten pence piece. Is there anything left alive in Regent's Park Zoo?

I don't like the way that man's slumped against that garage. Doubled up badly. Crumpled, green pyjamas. Do you change colour with radiation? Yes all the fucking colours of the rainbow. A flash and a fizzle. Out to black! An ashy orifice or two left; sirens crying for unburnt, white skin. Not old, beautiful sirens that called you onto the rocks. A single, hard one ordering your body into the relentlessly cracking earth! God I'm pissed! And the pyjamas are whimpering.

'You look sick. What's the matter?'

'It's my teeth.'

'It's not started. You can't have infected gums.'

'I've gone and lost a new pair of dentures. My daughter Ruth paid fifteen pounds for them. I've been ill. In bed for months. They kept the papers, TV and radio from me. Why did they go and leave me here alone? Must be something up. I don't like it. Weird. It's not the war is it?'

'No. Your daughter's just . . . gone to the country.'

'What's the day?'

'Sunday.'

'Sunday! She always stops with me then. If it's nice she walks me round Paddington recreation ground. What's she gone to the country for?'

'Fresh air.'

'There's fresh air at Paddington . . . oh God, those teeth were brand new!'

'I'll help you to find them.'

Crawling on all fours. An old face. Like a used-up, grey cotton reel on which time has badly wound back the thinning thread. Let me carry you back to bed. I'll rock you to sleep. Close your threadbare mouth.

*   *   *

'Will you tell Ruth something for me?'
  'What?'
  'Tell her they've got to be sterilised.'
  'I will.'
  'Promise, else I'll be sick on me soft crusts.'
  'I promise.'
  'Soft, soft crusts . . .'
  'Yes.'
  'Soft! So . . .'

Don't vanish old man. Don't fade away to leave your little, hunched-up shadow. Your teeth may be found after the war. When eating might be revived. All the billion shadows in the world won't unite you with your shadowy Ruth. Mine might be blown by the firestorm to Willesden Junction. Ah Celestine Salome Fergus! Might I not first rest my head against your bosom? Snuggle against your stone. Dream of holding your hand. Being sacrificed together in some shadowy car accident.

'Sorry, I've just locked up.'
  'But it's four hours to closing time!'
  'The dogs are scared. They know what's up.'
  'Please let me in. I want to be with my friends.'
  'Your friends are at home, sir.'
  'No. They're buried here. Can't you understand?'
  'A grown man befriending the dead. Look, sir, why don't you drive to the country. Be well out of it. I'm going home to hide in the cellar . . . did you hear that? They're wild now. Don't act like Securicor dogs any more . . . please don't climb over the gate. You'll only make them madder.'
  'I can't be harmed. The dead will protect me.'
  'Right sir. Have it your way then. But I'm off.'

There goes my whisky! Smashed on the road. Get off you stupid dogs! I'll call George Blunt of the Royal Fusiliers. Buried round the corner. Here George, here!

That's a good boy. Ram your musket up these beasts, will you?

'John, John. Over here!'
  'Henry . . . is that you?'
  'Yes.'
  'Where are you?'
  'By Clara Mercy's sepulchre!'
  It is Henry. My Hampstead priest.
  'God, these dogs!'

During the last great anti-war rallies, I remember being disturbed by a hint of cruel disbelief I perceived in a politician's face. He tried to efface it by smoothing back his hair. Yet the collapse of his look persisted. Especially as he stammered on the word 'agreement'. I knew he was lying. Nothing had been agreed. A year later the stammering increased. On his eyes was a miserable, giving-up film. In interviews, assurances of peace were too desperately sincere. Each blinking of the eye was further betrayal. I remember poking my fingers against the TV screen. Trying hard to blind him. I wrote to the newspapers. No one would print a piece on his TV looks. Last night he talked of 'preparation' without stammering. The film on the eyeballs had vanished. But there was the strong beginning of a double chin on his defeated face. He looked like a parody of Henry. I wanted him to snarl his pious gravity at us. Bark commands through a spiked dog collar.

'I'll continue my research till five to four. Then take a pill. Would you like one?'
  'I don't know, Henry.'
  'Quite right. Keep all options open!'
  'I think I'll come through.'
  'Pulverised he'll press on/Though all around the world has gone. Sorry about that doggerel! These cemetery inscriptions stick in the head. The only way you'll come through is as a particle. Part of the clean, orderly spread of dust and rubble.'

'I'd like to see your debris. Be a sole survivor. To say I'm the only one left alive. What a feeling!'

'Ah, let's save the two of us!'

'What would we do?'

'We could anoint ourselves with dust.'

'I'd want to move on.'

'Where?'

'Another place.'

'A place with a placename? You won't find one.'

'Shoreham-on-Sea. Smaller than London.'

'Doesn't mean it'll survive.'

'The epicentre grows.'

'Still, we could name them. Catalogue in our heads.'

'What?'

'The placenames.'

'Shoreham-on-Sea, Littlehampton, Rye, Lewes.'

'Our south-east kingdoms.'

'Signs and pointers.'

'For what . . . ?'

'Fixing us from going crazy.'

'We would be crazy. Naming places we couldn't go to. That didn't exist.'

'They might be around. But we'd never get through the wreckage of Kensal Green to find out.'

'Why are we talking like this?'

'Keeps your mind off the rubble.'

'No!'

'You're right. The old brain will be like ground pepper!'

A dark mortar and pestle scrunching the mind. Alien knights of the burning pestle: lancing the body sores of mortared Britain.

Henry's so worldly for a priest. A wonderful, inspiring irreverence. His confessional is a guiltless, comic banter. He abandoned his old priestly duties years ago. The approach of war threw out the institutionalised sacraments in his spirit. He returned to his great research – a book on funeral architecture. Unpurged Catholics were deserted. No relief from nuclear anxieties. The man was immersed in the structure of pyramids and catacombs. People were gently shuffled out of the church. Vague promises of listening later. Alone in his room, he'd laugh himself silly. Convinced that the warheads were God's angels shitting on the whole show. He didn't advertise the fact. Not like the media priests of the last few weeks. They were prone to humbly salivate the Revelation of John. The bit about an angel who was worthy to loosen the book's seven seals. This was regularly followed by a commercial for babies' nappies.

Funny, I feel a lot calmer now. And despite the scotch, a little more sober. Almost as if this mad reality had sunk in. *A light is from our households gone*. That's it. Simple. To the point. Thank you Frieda Clare – beloved wife of A. F. Goodlife. I desire nothing further from your proud, slim monument. The banality of your inscription touched me deeper than you'll ever know. The closer one gets to one's own time, the more that epitaphs lose their poetic charge. A lazy, manufactured torpidity. Stale references to dad or gran, the boring repetition of *In Loving Memory*, poor-quality headstones and a drastic reduction of decoration. It almost persuades me that a good case could be made out for cremation. Ashes in a pretty box. Stuffed into the back pocket of your denims. Kensal was built to be a grand, final home for mortal remains. Now it's a crowded, over-buried anachronism.

A rolling road to Kensal Green. It began to roll when I was quite small. I'd steal into my parents' room to look at my grandmother's photograph. Sandwiched between it and the album page was a frail ink drawing. There she was at sixteen attending her mother's funeral. Everyone was dressed in black crape. The artist had given it a peculiar sheen that despite the age of the drawing showed through. Grandmother was holding a black handkerchief to her face. Gradually I sensed that my roots, however dimly apprehended, were contained in the sketch. The crispy, crimpy appearance of the crape made me rush to my pencil and crayon box, I took out a piece of charcoal and stained my fingers till they were craped. Years later, I read in some obscure Victorian biography of a viscount's legs. It was on the day of a freakish heatwave. His thighs had been smudged black by sticky, crape trousers. He cried through the night, calling for his dead wife to sponge clean his flesh. As an adult I could understand him, no matter how morbid the need. But at the age of eight, I couldn't reconcile the pasty whiteness of a grief-stricken face with clothes so inexpressibly black. The violent contrast shook me. I wiped my hands on the drawing in order to return my charcoal memory to my descendants. I must have fainted because father took the album and picked up a . . .

'Steady . . . you're dizzy. You ought to lie down.'
    'I could do with another drink.'
    'Holocaust or not, I wouldn't touch the stuff!'
    'Need it to face father . . . the end . . . what can one believe in?'
    'That there's no god of love, that my buried manuscript, *Funeral Architecture of the World*, will be discovered and the warheads might be delayed.'
    'They'll be on time.'
    'Pity, I've still more corrections to make.'
    'May I give it a brief read – a scan?'
    'No time. I'm sorry.'
    'Christ I'm thirsty . . . my head aches . . .'
    'Lie down. Here by the canal.'

He was one of the most able and successful of public servants. Colonel Sir William De Bothebart. I could pull his cord and ask room service to send up a drink. What cord? The chipped one on his marble shroud. You called, sir? Yes, my guests and I require more refreshments. Yes, sir. And find out why it's so stuffy in this hotel!

The water and a warm sun. Fine weather for mid-spring. I ought to take off my tracksuit. So hot and smelly. Fall asleep. What about the strike? It's just after three. Go

on, doze awhile. Henry will wake me up when it's time.
We'll hold each other for comfort by the mausoleum of
the Molyneux family. Resplendent, Gothic octagon of
the 1860s.

*Of course democracy will have to go by the board for
a while.* That county controller on the radio phone-in. *A
posthumous defence!* His advice to high-rise flat dwellers
was to inhabit the lower storeys. My old, deaf mother:
grossly overweight and weeping on her lower floor. Hiding
under the kitchen table like she did when she heard a bad
clap of thunder. Get out! Quickly! Take your chances
outdoors. *What an escape from the choked charnel house to
that verdant wide expanse* . . . Ainsworth Magazine (1882)
on Kensal Green . . . verdant expanse? . . . just a wide old
space . . . where one can rest awhile.

The old man found his dentures. They had fallen under his
bed. Been kicked to the back of the dirty skirting board.
Blowing off the fluff, he reset them on his moaning gums.
He knew that war was coming. The old man was glad Ruth
had kept him in the dark. She'd have none of his screaming
panic to contend with. Ruth, Dan and the children came
first. So long as they were out of it.

He put on his glasses and looked down the deserted
street. It was more Sunday than Sunday. The only person he'd met was a helpful, tracksuited man. *I couldn't
have dreamt him*, he thought. *Else how did I get back
upstairs?*

He remembered tearing his pyjamas on a nail in the
gate. He fingered the hole in the green cotton. A paucity of
hair on his wounded knee made him smile. Palm cupping
the flesh, he limped back to his sagging mattress. Just
before closing his eyes, he glimpsed an image of a burnt
daughter kissing his knee. He screamed. She flung an
arm round his neck and tried to make him drink some
disinfectant. She burnt even more: determined that her
blazing body console her father. He struggled to unloosen
her fierce grip, crying that he'd face it alone.

Large, blackened feet. His crabbed toes melted. No part of the earth left for him to scuttle his independence.

Henry's last Biro had run out. There were still two paragraphs to correct. The manuscript was a bulky affair. The chapter on our time, *Tributes of a tragic memorialist*, had caused him problems. He wished he'd been able to insert at least one positive statement. The book's conclusion was dispiriting. The vandalising of cemeteries, cremation, the ugly haste of last rites and neglect of ritual. All were examples of a brutish flight from death.

He thought hard of a redemptive sentence. Neither pretentious nor trite. Noble without being condescending. Lucid but still suggesting doubt. It refused to come. There was nothing for it but to bury the manuscript. *But where? And how deep? What can I dig with?* The shock wave would create a burning crater. Henry clung to the irrational fancy that the book would live on. Some inviolable A4 space singled out to give immunity from Fahrenheit 451. One religiously researched written world amidst the unscholarly, destroyed outer. Henry stuffed the pages down his trouser waist. Rested against his belly, he instructed the warmth of his skin to ward off the greater, approaching heat.

His watch said twenty past four. *My God, they're terribly late!*

He touched John's shoulder. The difficult sentence wrote itself. Henry saw a pen in John's tracksuit pocket. The flash blinded him. He wrote defiantly on the air.

John's dreaming now. Dreaming of an icy-cold river carrying him to another shore. Strong currents speed out from the canal. Penetrate the ocean. The fires on the land have been doused. Other smaller bodies (his children . . . and now his wife) have joined him. You yell to them. They open their blistered mouths and softly cry, 'The heather was burnt!' The ocean is littered with rescued shrubs. You greedily chew some till a feeling of renewal is digested. Hold hands to this feeling. Pray that fires will not start on the water. That you can all keep afloat.

On the ocean bed are sunken forms. Pillars, roofs, spires and broken headstones. A lone dog floats up entangled on a notice. Kensal Green is below you, John. Roll down to confront its peace. Pocket this Victorian Atlantis. Scratch your family's name on a stone.

Under the fairy lights

Judy Hines

Judy Hines was born in May 1961 in Canterbury. She wrote her first story in 1985 when she was living in Pontoise, north of Paris. She returned to England and the story came second in a West Midlands writing competition. It was later included in a booklet of prize-winning entries entitled Inside City Walls.

Currently working as receptionist for a firm of chartered accountants, most of her spare time is devoted to writing her first novel, whose title is 'ever changing' and subject matter 'hard to describe'. When pushed she reveals only that it's 'very peculiar'. She lists her influences as Michel Tournier, Marie Cardinal and Dostoevsky.

Intriguing.

She also scours secondhand record shops and takes an interest in astronomy and drawing. At present she lives somewhere east of London.

Judy Hines's style, at least in Under the Fairy Lights, *is elliptical and those things left out are as important as those left in. As for the details which are present, the reader will establish the link between them. There's something terribly sad, for instance, about someone who lives on the fourteenth floor and watches* Gardeners' World. *The story is rather like a large-scale map of a small, unknown country and, like any map, if you read it closely enough, you feel you are there.*

Under the fairy lights

From the very beginning I hated the city. It was nothing but concrete and dirt. From up there on the fourteenth floor, all I could see of the countryside were little green squares in the distance. For the first few days, I spent my time staring out of the window, doing nothing.

Peter was worried about me, I could tell, and he didn't know what to do. He would give me money; anything I wanted. So I took the money and bought myself some binoculars, a zoom-lens camera, a pile of books. Things began to get better. By the fifth day, I felt brighter. That evening, when he came home, I'd even hoovered the carpets and made some dinner, which was a step in the right direction, he said. He was very good to me really, very patient. The dinner wasn't much, in fact, just a salad really, but he didn't complain; he just smiled at me and squeezed my hand.

Half an hour at the window, then I would wash up; it only took a bit of self-discipline. Then peel the potatoes, then watch *Gardeners' World*; life would be so much better with a video. But no brooding, be strong; turn the switch, wash a shirt, maybe two. What about getting a budgerigar? Perhaps.

He bought me a budgerigar; I was so grateful. But when he'd kissed me goodbye and gone off to work I cried; it

Judy Hines

was in a cage, and it was blue. He'd tried, but he couldn't really know.

I caught a bus, a long, long way. Through the busy streets, the big buildings, off towards the smaller ones, to the village. There was a field, then another, it all turned to one big field; budgie sang, and for some reason my eyes were still dry.

Out of the bus, into the cool wet air; something was wrong. The fields here were brown, black, not as they should be. Peter would wonder where I was. The light was going, it was September, and budgie's cage felt heavy in my hands. We went home then; there was always a bus into the city, not long to wait.

Peter had been worried; he hadn't expected me to go out. He put his finger under my chin, lifted my face up to his in search of an explanation. I don't really know whether or not he found it, but he chose not to question me further, and told me instead about his day.

I listened, straining to make sense of what he was saying. I wanted to understand, and share in his problems and pre-occupations, because I really loved him. I hadn't loved him since the day we first met; I hadn't really grown to love him properly until very recently. In our early days things had all been very different; we were nothing much, just suits, cars, briefcases full of petty worries, red wine in the evenings and then so much laughter. We were nothing more than a coincidence; I remember how Peggy had laughed when I said that to her, much later, when we'd chosen the ring and set the date. She said I was an incurable romantic; but she'd had too much wine as well.

Peggy bought a new car and married a Frenchman; they didn't talk to each other very much, it seemed. Peter and I did well for ourselves really; his business flourished, and we moved out of our terrace in Muswell Hill and bought a brand-new bungalow, in Sunbury-on-Thames, I think it was. I got put up to a better position at work, which helped with paying for it. When we moved in we had a big party; food and fairy lights in the garden. All very nice.

94

Peter had realised I wasn't listening to him any more. This time his patience seemed to go; he got up and went into the kitchen; I heard the fridge door, then a clink and a hiss as he opened a can of beer. He wasn't angry, I knew, just sad; I was right, because he came and kissed me goodnight before going to bed.

I met Martin under the fairy lights, in the cool, damp September air. He was wearing a dinner jacket, and he was drunk. He told me I had beautiful breasts, and that he was a friend of Peter's. I believed him.

The day after the party, Peter took me to his parents' house for tea. I remember I wasn't really in the mood. I kept thinking about Martin, wondering when I would see him again. I saw him soon enough. He was waiting for me outside my office, on the Monday night, a big bunch of red roses in his hand. I'd always loved roses. He told me again that he was a friend of Peter's, but this time I didn't believe him. He didn't mention my breasts again until later on that night. By then, I'd stopped worrying about Peter.

I had to face him the following morning, though, and it was then that I realised what I'd done. I wished that I hadn't gone with Martin. He had lost the appeal he had had under the fairy lights, and I could see Peter didn't believe the lie I told him about a friend going into hospital. I'd thrown the roses away in the park, but the bin was overflowing and they had all spilled out onto the path.

What did Martin do to me, I wonder? I've never really understood it. But after that night, whenever I touched Peter, I felt strange, incomplete, not really human any more. Like a little child, wanting a cuddle, a punishment, anything rather than the secret guilt hidden away for ever. Sometimes, I was sure I could hear Peter crying softly in the bathroom, when he thought I was asleep. I phoned Martin and told him I wouldn't see him any more, ever, and that I loved Peter. He didn't believe me.

The following day he phoned me at work and I put the phone down. He sent me some more roses, and

I determinedly took them to the park and this time threw them in the lake. That seemed more appropriate somehow. I phoned Martin and told him what I'd done, that it was final. This time he hung up.

Suddenly budgie started to sing and I didn't know why. It was dark and his cage was all covered up. Didn't he know that birds aren't supposed to sing when it's dark? He was a stupid bird. Why had Peter bought me a stupid budgie? Perhaps because he thought we'd get on well together; perhaps it hadn't been kindness after all.

No. Peter loved me. I loved Peter, I didn't deserve all this kindness. I wanted to be good, I wanted to love my budgerigar. I got up and uncovered the cage, and spoke softly to the little blue bird inside. I reached into the cage and took him in my hands. But something went wrong. I loved him too much; I crushed him.

Then Peter was there, holding me in his arms, and telling me not to worry. He would take care of me. He would find a place for me, he knew things were all getting too much for me lately, he would take me far away from the flat, from the city, out to a nice quiet place in the country where all was green and lovely the way I liked it. He would even give me a present before I went, he'd been saving it for me, he said. He let go of me and walked over to the sideboard, unlocked it and took out a little box. I took it from him and began to open it, my eyes still clouded with tears for budgie and love for Peter.

Inside the box was a mouldy, slushy mess, a smell of rotting vegetation, fetid water, dead flowers. I didn't understand.

Pavlov's wristwatch

Philip Nutman

Philip Nutman was born in London in 1963. He was raised in Bath, where he made short movies (some of which were shown at the Hong Kong Film Festival), read vast quantities of horror fiction, went for long country walks and started writing. In 1982 he returned to London and worked for four years at BBC TV before becoming a full-time writer.

He published his first non-fiction at 15 and since then has sold more than 200 feature articles and interviews to magazines as diverse as Penthouse, Twilight Zone, The New York Times, Cable Guide, L'Ecran Fantastique, Premiere *and* Spin. *As British correspondent for* Fangoria *magazine – and later American correspondent for* Fear *magazine – he covered most of the major horror films of the 1980s, while starting to write screenplays. His first short story,* Wet Work, *appeared in Skipp and Spector's* Book of the Dead *anthology in 1989, and forms the basis of his first novel, due soon from Berkley.*

Currently living in the US, he acted in the low-budget video feature Death Collector *and I can report that his performance is definitely the main attraction (any offer over £2.50 secures my copy). Off-screen he works for Tundra Publishing in Northampton, Mass., and continues to write powerful fiction. He contributed a story to* Nightmares on Elm Street: Freddy Krueger's Seven Sweetest Dreams, *and his* Full Throttle *was one of the highlights of the* Splatterpunks *anthology. In* Pavlov's Wristwatch *he takes us to a wet and windy Finchley, and beyond into uncharted psychotic territory.*

Pavlov's wristwatch

As soon as the tube train entered the tunnel Hatchard felt uncomfortable.

The sudden rush of rotten air made his ears pop and, as he swallowed to clear them, he felt the crowded compartment close in. Sweat began to pool under his arms making his blue polyester shirt stick to his skin. He tried to breathe shallowly to conserve oxygen, but this did little to reduce the smells attacking his nose.

A garlic pong clouded the carriage, coming from a portly man to his right. He hoped the man would get off soon; he hated the smell of garlic. The smell swirled around him, clashing with the sickly sweet smell of perfume coming from the woman on his left. Fortunately, as the train pulled into Highgate station, the woman, her face a mask of Max Factor, stood up to squeeze her way towards the doors. As she went a youth in a tattered denim jacket slipped into the vacant seat. He was wearing a Walkman, noise overflowing from the headset that looked to Hatchard like an Aliceband with tiny earmuffs. He began to bite his already ragged nails, gnawing at the quicks.

With a jolt the train lurched as it quickly departed from the station, throwing him against the portly man.

'I'm sorry,' he mumbled, but the man ignored him.

The youth placed a new tape in the machine, tapping his foot to the staccato beat hissing from the headset.

Tick . . . tick . . . tick . . . tick, tick, tick . . .

Hatchard's throat went dry. The clock-like noise, steady, relentless, unnerved him. He tried to push the thought from his mind but it was no good, it had already taken root. Try as he might to imagine something nice (a dish of ice cream, yes, a big dish of raspberry ripple crowned with a maraschino cherry and wafer fan) the face of the Crocodile bled through the melting confectionary. It was taunting him. It couldn't come for him here, not with so many people around. You couldn't be taken by the Crocodile in such a place, could you?

How could it?

Could it?

But the Crocodile was the Crocodile. It knew more than he. There was so much he didn't know or understand. He suddenly felt very cold.

Tick, tick, tick . . . tick, tick, tick . . .

He squashed his eyelids to shut out the world and began to mumble his prayer.

'I am a free man. I do not believe in clocks. Clocks are BAD. I am free of time. My time isn't up yet because it doesn't exist. I'm free. Crocodile you cannot touch me.'

Against the black screen of his squeezed eyes the Crocodile leered its greedy grin, opening its mouth, the echo of the clock that beat in its sepulchral belly teasing him.

Tick, tick, tick . . . tick, tick, tick . . .

He continued to scrunch his eyes until they hurt as he repeated the prayer, more forcefully this time. Still the clock sound continued to chip away at his nerves.

The train arrived at Archway. Some people got off. Many more boarded. Why didn't the youth leave? Oh, please make him stop! He opened his eyes in panic. Didn't the other passengers realise what the youth was doing – calling the Crocodile, playing its game? No. They were fools. Isolated fools. Blind. Unaware of the huge shape lurking behind them, dogging their every step, pretending nothing mattered except getting to work. As he looked around he saw no one was taking any notice of him, were unaware of the seriousness of their situation, the idiots. That, of course, was what the Crocodile wanted. Not him, not just Stephen Hatchard – it wanted them all. And the youth was calling it with his tapping. Now he knew the awful truth. Somewhere ahead of the train the Crocodile lay in the tunnel, its body grown huge on the dead flesh of others. Then he thought the train could be inside the Crocodile, the tunnel its throat, their destination the cavernous belly.

No, how could it?

His imagination was running away, trying to take him with it, trying to take him to the Crocodile. But he wouldn't go! He was a FREE MAN.

As the train pulled into Tufnell Park there came a beeping sound and the portly man tugged up the sleeve of his raincoat to consult a digital watch.

This was too much! He stood up, jostling a man reading *The Times*, pushing against the newspaper.

'Watch it,' the man said.

Hatchard whimpered as he squirmed his way towards the doors. 'Stupid git,' someone else moaned as he pushed frantically forward to reach the platform before the doors closed.

'Manners,' said a woman as he shoved her in desperation.

'Excuse me, excuse me,' he mumbled, remembering manners maketh man, even in the face of death.

There! He'd made it. He was out!

His breath came in short gasps which attracted the appalled attention of a young woman rummaging in her handbag as he leapt out in front of her. He smiled sheepishly but she backed away, disturbed by his unkempt appearance. He began to trot towards the stairs. It had been a silly, no, *dangerous* idea to take the tube into central London. He should have known better and taken the bus. Relieved by his escape, he grinned a Cheshire cat grin to himself as he reached the flight of steps.

* * *

Rain started to fall steadily as he trudged up Ballard's Lane towards home, prompting him to quicken his pace. The sky had been low and heavily overcast all morning, pregnant with a promised downpour that had finally come to term, falling like the tears of God, washing away the encrusted scabs of litter choking the gutters. He slipped his father's books inside his army surplus coat, pulled the frayed collar around his ears, and lowered his head against the water.

father would be cross if there was the faintest damp mark on the books so he stopped under a depleted tree, its leaves taken by the unusually strong autumn winds they'd had of late, repositioning the brown paper bag containing the books beneath his worn Harris tweed jacket. It was still a ways to the old Victorian house and rain was now descending in icy sheets. Better he catch a cold than return home with wet books.

The traffic lights were green at the junction with Sunningdale Road. Cars sped past, travelling too fast for the weather conditions, and as he stood by the kerb one hit a puddle, sending a small wave over his trousers. He groaned. The lights seemed to stay green for longer than usual, two emerald eyes staring at him. At this rate the books would get wet if he took his usual route. Since he was a free man he decided to go another way, hoping to speed his journey. He turned left into Long Lane, trotting now, trying to avoid the cracks between the paving stones. After a while he was drenched but could see the rooftops of Squires Lane and HOME. He was a CLEVER BOY. If mummy were still alive she would have told him so.

Though she had been dead for many moons (the only way he could gauge forward movement was via the lunar cycles, because they were natural, like the passing of the seasons and his father felt that was the way things should be) he still missed her. When she had been pleased with him he was rewarded with a dish of ice cream or a plate of Jaffa cakes. Now, whenever he ate them, he thought of her. But on those times she thought him a BAD BOY, he'd been sent to his room. He'd never questioned his punishment. mummy was always right. 'You are FREE but you have to learn,' she used to say. That had been mummy's responsibility, to teach him the things he needed to know. Of course it was, she'd been a teacher before she got A-GRO-PH-OB-I-A and was confined to the house. Yes, he missed her, even though he was now an adult, could take care of himself, and more importantly could eat ice cream whenever he wished.

Rounding the corner he realised he was by the cinema. This was fortunate as the Finchley Odeon had a large awning jutting from its front. He crossed the road to stop beneath it, looking intently at the bright colours of the film posters.

The Odeon was a large old cinema that, in his childhood, had had one huge screen. mummy used to take him there whenever there was something she thought suitable, which wasn't often. But moons ago it had been turned into one with three screens. Standing outside the grey, worn building, he tried to recall the last time he'd visited the picture house, but he couldn't remember. He mainly watched films on television.

One screen had a film called *Platoon*. The poster showed a man on his knees, arms out in a V, his head back as if crying out to the heavens asking the rain to stop. It looked like a war film. He liked war films but mummy had disapproved. They were violent and evil, she said. War was BAD. Maybe he'd come and see it if the rain stopped and father fell asleep early. The second film had a scary-looking film called *Hellraiser*, and he shuddered as he looked at a poster showing a piece of flesh pulled back on a hook. He didn't like scary films. They frightened him and the world was so big it was already scary enough. He moved to look at the third screen – and froze.

No! Not again!

It . . . it . . . was too much. First the terrifying experience on the tube, and now this. The Crocodile was playing with him, taunting him like a cat with a mouse. There on the poster was the beast itself, leering its evil, knowing smile, the eyes narrowed to slits as it licked its lips as it menaced the Pirate. The shock of the image made him lose his grip on the books beneath his coat; they fell to the pavement with a heavy slap, making him start from his transfixed state. Stooping to lift them from the ground he did not take his eyes from the poster. Was it a trick of the light as his angle of vision altered, or did the Crocodile wink at him? Of course it was no optical illusion, the reptile was filled with cunning. It winked again, saying silently *you are mine*. He couldn't stand there any longer; every part of him felt touched by cold, wet fingers. He turned to run, gasping as he collided with a tall, grey-haired man. He squealed piglet-like and bounded across the road, narrowly missing a red Vauxhall Chevette, the tall man watching, a concerned expression on his face.

As he reached the other side he dared look back. The tall man was still watching him, then turned to the movie poster. The angle of light on the plastic covering obscured the Crocodile's image, cutting the poster in two. It was gone. All he could see as he disappeared around the corner was the film's title:

Peter Pan.

He shivered in the porch, fumbling for his keys. He found them and opened the door. Slamming it against the cold and wet he sneezed.

'Stephen?' his father called from upstairs, the sound that of fingernails on a chalk board. He moved slowly up the tall, shadowy flight of stairs, the top cloaked in darkness.

'Yes, father.'

The elderly man was propped up in bed, his frail frame cradled by three pillows. As usual the reading light was on, throwing an orange slash across the blanket on which lay a pile of books.

'Did you get them?' father asked in a hushed tone.

He nodded, offering the soggy bag.

'Ach! Look at you!' the old man said. 'My books! Go dry them, then yourself. The books first!'

'I'm s-s-sorry, father, I'm – '

'Go dry them!'

He turned and headed for the bathroom. 'And bring me a glass of water,' the old man added, his request punctuated by a coughing fit.

After he wiped the books and brought father the water, he changed into clean clothes in his room, leaving the wet trousers in a tangled heap on the bare boards alongside other piles of dirty laundry and a strewn selection of magazines: *Newsweek*, *The Plain Truth*, *Harper's*, *The Face*, *Country Living*, *Cosmopolitan*. He'd found them neatly tied with string next to the dustbin at number 57 a few days before, rescuing them before the dustmen took them away. Magazines held his attention better than books because of the photos. Even if he didn't understand the articles (*The Plain Truth* was clear enough though; that one said the world was coming to an end, and he knew it was the Crocodile's doing) the pictures provided him with endless interesting discoveries. Like something called the G spot, a man who looked like a pretty girl but was called Boy George, and the President of America was an old actor who once appeared in a film with a monkey called Bonzo.

He sneezed again as he looked at them. It was still raining so there was little chance of a trip to the cinema. Not that he could go there with the Crocodile waiting so close. Once he was in the dark he knew it would get him.

Aware he was hungry, he sneezed again and started for the stairs.

Although it was HOME, the gloomy hallway was ripe with hidden menace. He hated passing the collection of skulls on top of the bookshelves, their vacant eyesockets black, mysterious. But he liked looking at mummy's books, old volumes by people called Hardy, Dickens, Trollope, Christie, and the children's stories by E. Nesbit she used to read him. *Five Children and It* was his favourite. Then there were father's books. Non-fiction. Volumes by Skinner, Pavlov, Watson, Hull, Freud, and Ellis, and many, many others – SERIOUS WORKS father called them. He'd tried to read them once but couldn't understand the words; all he knew was they were PSYCHO-LOGY books because that's what father was – a PSYCHO-LOGIST, or had been until his accident.

He trod carefully down the stairs. Some creaked and the sound scared him. He might fall. He went to the kitchen once he safely reached the bottom.

All the refrigerator had to offer was some soup from the day before and a piece of cheese. He'd have to go shopping but didn't like the idea of getting wet again. But there was ice cream in the freezer section. He smiled, then sneezed again. He sat at the table, digging in. Neopolitan. Not as good as raspberry.

He looked out of the window. Rain was pelting down now, the sky low, very dark.

(Like the night mummy died)

The rain was pounding the flowers on her grave and he frowned. He would have to get more as he hated the sight of the earthen mound without their pretty petals giving the ground a splash of colour. mummy had loved flowers so much. father said it was a waste. Still, he tended the grave with loving care, just the way mummy would have done.

Drip . . . drip . . . drip . . .

He shuddered. The tap was leaking, making hollow sounds in the sink.

Drip . . . drip . . . drip . . .

Watch noise again.

He rushed over to turn it off. The handle was stiff, wouldn't turn any further, and he grumbled to himself.

Drip . . . drip . . . drip . . .

No! He hated the sound. Ticking. Time had no place in the house. father said so and he was always right, that's why there were no clocks.

(I AM A FREE MAN!)

The wind rattled the window pane. Outside, a gust lifted the rain-lashed roses from the sodden earth, spreading yellow petals over the overgrown lawn.

Drip . . . drip . . . drip . . .

He couldn't listen to the sound, he'd have t –

'Stephen!' father suddenly shrieked from upstairs, making him jump, making him drop the bowl of ice cream. It shattered into four pieces on the cracked red linoleum.

'Stephen!'

He ran from the kitchen.

Drip . . . drip . . . drip . . .

Up the stairs.

Creak . . . creak . . . creak . . .

His father's face was red with rage.

'Look!' the old man cried, his long beard jerking, spittle flying from his lips as he held up one of the books, a rare copy of Fodor and Katz's *The Structure of Language*.

'Look, you simpleton!'

The edges were damaged, probably as a result of dropping the books. But there was more. Worse. The inside of the back cover was marked by a stain, still damp.

'I'm . . . m . . . m . . . s-s-s-s-sorry, f-father,' he mumbled, trying to control his stutter.

'Come here!'

He shuffled towards the bed, knew what was coming.

father reached for the birch rod he kept beside the bed.

Stephen hesitated.

'Here.'

No. Not the rod. Please, not the rod again!

'Stephen! You – you cringing son of a whore.'

It was no good. He stepped to the bed and extended his left hand.

The rod came down. Hard.

The first blow stung.

The second made his hand feel like it did the time he burned it on the cooker.

The third made him cry out.

'Shut up!'

father went to hit him again and he pulled back.

'Whoreson!'

The old man suddenly pushed himself away from the pillows, his speed belying his aged frailty. The blow caught him across the face. He squealed, feeling his left eye flinch with the pain.

Then father began to gasp. Deep, agonising gasps as his asthmatic lungs tried to pull in air. He clutched desperately at his pyjama top, dropping the rod on the bed, trying to reach the respirator on the bedside table. Books, the empty glass and the respirator went flying.

'Help . . . me!' father gasped.

Stephen stood still, his hand burning, his face throbbing, eye smarting from the blow.

'Help . . . me . . .' a whisper this time.

He moved, scampering for the respirator, thrusting it into father's hands. The old man pressed the button, the oxygen hissing into his mouth as he collapsed back onto the pillows.

Stephen stood there, afraid to move, to speak, tears running down his cheeks.

The Crocodile! It was the Crocodile's fault! It had scared him, made him drop the books.

father wheezed for a while, but his breathing eventually steadied. The old man looked at him with contempt.

'Look . . . look what you caused, boy. You want me to die?' Stephen shook his head – no. 'You fool. I was cursed the day you crawled from your mother's womb.' father paused. 'I wanted a son, a son who could continue my work. What did I get? An imbecile. Don't look at me with those pitiful eyes – your mother's eyes. Not mine! Just like her – weak.' He wheezed. 'The sight of you makes me sick.'

father turned away.

He stood there terrified, his stomach churning with hurt and fear.

'Go.'

Stephen turned, shuffling, heading for his room. Outside, a huge gust of wind pushed against the house and as he went down the long dark hallway he could hear the trees tapping against the bathroom window. He'd gone but a few feet when father called his name again. He went back to the bedroom.

'My books,' the old man said. Stephen picked up the volumes lying on the floor, copies of *Behaviourism, Beyond Freedom and Dignity*, and Chomsky's *Language and the Mind*, placing them neatly on the bed.

'Good boy,' father said softly.

Another gust beat against the house, the branches of the elm outside father's room tap, tap, tapping forcefully against the window like the fingers of an old man seeking sanctuary from the storm. father ignored the noise, settling back into his pillows, closing his eyes.

Stephen went to his room. Stepping over the pile of magazines he threw himself on the bed, sobbing as he crawled beneath the dirty blankets, pulling them around him as he tucked himself into a ball.

Eventually he slept.

He awoke in the dark to a steady roar of rain on the roof, rhythmic sprays against the window. His face hurt. His hand hurt. His stomach groaned with hunger. After listening to the rain until he felt totally lost like the little boy he'd read about who'd survived a sinking ship only to spend five nights adrift on the ocean, he crawled from the bed deciding to eat the soup.

Drip . . . drip . . . drip . . .

The tap continued to taunt him but he decided he was going to eat the soup hot instead of cold and lit the gas stove. The wind continued to lash the rain against the windows, drowning out the dripping noise.

'mummy,' he said, 'I wish you were here.'

109

Tears, silent this time, fell as he stirred the soup. His left hand was red and swollen, and his eyelid, bruised, nearly covered his eye, reminding him of the Pirate.

(Crocodile)

Dread lay on his shoulders, rounded despite his 20 years, like a heavy overcoat.

'mummy.'

Drip . . . drip . . . drip . . .

It was no good, the tap was too much. He poured the barely warm soup into a dirty bowl and went to the lounge where he wouldn't be able to hear it.

The television was an old black and white Ferguson set he'd also discovered in the street on one of his seek-and-ye-shall-find missions. mummy and father never allowed one in the house when she was alive, but with father bedridden, he didn't know he had one. He switched it on, turning the volume up so there was no chance of hearing the tap.

BBC1 was showing the news.

Boring. ITV had a quiz show.

Maybe.

But BBC2 was showing a wildlife programme. He smiled faintly. He liked wildlife programmes. mummy said they were WHOLESOME. Like those Disney films she took him to.

(Crocodile)

He gritted his teeth.

(go away)

David Attenborough was in Egypt walking across sand, pyramids jutting up into the sky behind him like upside-down ice cream cones.

Lightning lit the sky through the lounge windows. The picture jumped. Seconds later thunder crashed. He whimpered.

A storm.

Like the one the day he'd buried mummy.

David Attenborough was talking about scorpions and the television showed one on the sand attacking a bird, its tail flicking out – once, twice – the bird jerking, then flopping on the ground.

A flash. The picture went fuzzy.

He spooned up the last of the soup, set the bowl on the worn green carpet and hugged himself, shivering.

(mummy)

(why is mummy cold?)

He would never forget the day the Crocodile came for her. It had been a few days after she'd taken him to see *Peter Pan*.

Like this morning, the day had started sunny, though warmer because spring was coming. father had been more withdrawn than usual, poring over his books while propped up in bed, and barely acknowledged their presence when they brought him lunch.

The afternoon passed quietly. He built a Lego house, coloured in one of his colouring books, read a Bugs Bunny comic. Later he fell asleep, curled up on the couch. The BAD DREAMS came again.

It started after seeing *Peter Pan*. In the dream he was walking. Never running, always walking, his legs stiff. The dream world was dark, empty ground like the old land beside the petrol station at the East Finchley end of Long Lane. Something was coming. Something was out there in the dark. When he looked he couldn't see it. But he knew it was there. The dream – mummy said they were NIGHTMARES – would end when he reached a sudden brick wall without end. He would cry on waking.

This time he awoke to the sound of his mummy's screams.

He thought he was still dreaming, but the persistence of the sound pulled him from the womb of sleep, aware his father was shouting – angry, unpleasant words. Even if their meanings were unclear the tone of voice was not. Then it changed. mummy stopped screaming and father, he realised, was shouting for help. He ran to the bedroom.

She lay on the floor, her neck a lump of purple bruises,

her green eyes bulging. father was on the floor too, as if a giant had picked up the bed, tossing him to the floor like a thin wooden doll, his withered legs poking from his pyjamas, the stumps of his ankles pointing to mummy's body, two fingers without nails.

He cried out, bending over her twisted body. What was wrong?

(mummy)

father started shouting again, demanding to be put back in bed. Stephen ignored him. mummy. What's wrong with mummy?

He held her hand. It was limp. Help me, father shouted, adding, she's dead.

(ded)

How?

It took her, father said. The Crocodile came for her. Came to take her away. I stopped it. But the shock killed her.

He cried. Hoarse, desperate sobs that made his chest hurt as he cradled her body in his lap, father glaring at him.

Later, after he had placed father back in bed and carried mummy downstairs to lay her on the couch, he smashed all the plates and glasses in the kitchen, fear and sorrow giving way to a TEMPER TANTRUM, only this time mummy didn't send him to his room because she was DED – and that meant he didn't have a mummy any more.

father, surprisingly, didn't complain about the noise from the kitchen. Later, when Stephen was calmer, he told him to bury her in the garden by nightfall. Then it started raining suddenly as black clouds covered the sun and he froze as he looked out of the window because

(Crocodile)

one cloud looked like a giant one cloud looked like a troll but the other one the other one looked like looked like

(Crocodile)

the Crocodile.

It rained. And rained, turning the garden into a sea of mud.

Darkness fell.

He couldn't sleep. He sat in the armchair looking at mummy lying there as rain drummed on the roof, rolling down the windows like a flood of tears.

When he went to move her mummy had turned a grey colour and beneath the smell of lavender water

(do you like the smell of mummy's perfume stephen?)

she smelled like the old carpet he had once found in the street, soggy and rotten.

He buried her and then the truth sank in: she was gone.

The Crocodile had taken her.

As he finished packing the topsoil down it started to rain again, but lightly, not with the scary force of the previous night's storm.

Tonight, so many moons since then, the storm sounded like it was directly over the house as a crash of thunder made the windows shake. Then the television and the lights went out. He whimpered and started reciting the PRAYER.

'I am a FREE MAN. I do not believe in clocks. Clocks are BAD.

(the watch)

I am free of time.

(that was a SECRET)

My time isn't up because it doesn't exist.

(his SECRET)

I am free. Crocodile you can not touch me.'

Lightning flashed, illuminating the corners of the room. Shapes moved. SECRET things. Creatures he couldn't see in the dark. But they could see him, oh yes, old things. Rotting things. Ded things. CROCODILE things.

'You cannot touch me!'

(could it?)

Lightning.

The things in the corner moved again.

Thunder crash.

'Go away!'

The lights came on. He shouted with surprise, jerking on the couch. Then the television picture stuttered to life and David Attenborough was standing beside a big river.

' – but perhaps most regal of Egyptian wildlife is the crocodile,' he was saying, the picture changing to film of logs in the water. Only they weren't logs they were – crocodiles!!

He shrieked and ran to the television set, twisting the on/off knob so hard it came off in his hand. He ran back to the couch and pulled himself into a ball, arms tightly clasped around his legs.

It was here! He knew it.

He held himself so tightly his arms ached and his legs were seized by cramp. His eye throbbed, his hand was stiff and his nose was running. The beast was here. It was in the house. It had been playing with him, taunting him and now –

Lightning.

The lights flickered then died.

Thunder crashed.

No! No! No! Nonononononononon . . .

A slow roar came from outside the front of the house, long and low like the noise the dinosaurs made in the cartoons. The sound of glass shattering came from upstairs. father cried out, a terrible screaming wail that cut off –

Then . . .

Then nothing.

He pulled his arms around his head, crying, whimpering. mummymummymummymummymummymummy –

A shout. Weak. Dying.

Then just the sound of the rain.

It had come. It was here.

The Crocodile

Lightning. Fainter this time.

He peered through his fingers. His left eye was almost

closed now and he couldn't see properly. But the things were still there, were closer, moving out of the corners, closing in on him.

'father!'

He bolted from the couch

(father!)

collided with the coffee table, knocked it over, nearly fell himself. He ran for the stairs, tripped, fell, landed heavily on his left hand and cried out.

'father!'

Thunder rumbled.

He reached the top of the stairs, turning towards father's room. Shadows had turned into black curtains that seemed to hang from the walls to cover the floor. The hallway had grown longer too. Now it seemed to stretch before him like a narrow passageway, its size not right, the open doorway leading to father's room a small shape standing out, dark, but lighter than the walls.

'father?'

Nothing, only the soft roaring of the rain.

One step. Two steps. Three steps. He started down the hallway. *It's not real, it's not real, it's not real.* It's just the hallway. A hallway with bookshelves and books and

(skulls)

(ded things)

Just a hallway

(rotting things)

just the hallway, and at the end father would be sitting in bed waiting for the lights to come on.

'father?' Almost a whisper.

Seven steps. Eight steps. Nine steps.

He had to see. He had to reach father.

Twelve steps. Thirteen steps.

'I am a FREE MAN. Crocodile, you cannot touch me.'

He stepped into the doorway.

Lightning flashed, blinding him.

When his eyes adjusted he screamed. A long, hysterical screeching painful scream as he turned to run for his bedroom.

The Crocodile's shape was halfway through the window, its massive head and shoulders on the bed, *on father*, as it ate him up.

He ran, knocking against the bookshelves, crashing into the opposite wall as he raced for the door, hitting it so hard with his full weight he nearly threw it off its hinges. He slammed it behind him, skidding on the magazines underfoot, his breath coming in frantic huffing-puffing-blow-your-house-down gasps as he pulled the chest of drawers away from the wall with his good hand, dragging it against the door, sliding down to the floor with his back against the hard knobs.

The darkness was DARK.

Light. He must have light!

(torch)

His torch! Where was it?

He turned, pulling out the bottom drawer, pulling screwed-up shirts, twisted pairs of trousers.

The torch. His hand touched it, his thumb rubbing the button like a magic spot.

Light.

He sighed. Light was GOOD.

And –

And he couldn't hear the Crocodile. But it was out there. It knew where he was, and once it had finished with father it would come for him. He felt safer now he had the light. Maybe he could blind it and escape. No, no that was no good. The Crocodile would get him. What could he do?

(watch)

He sneezed.

(??thewatch??)

The watch!

(SECRET)

Yes, *his* SECRET. The watch he had found on one of his seek-and-ye-shall-find walks around the neighbourhood. The little old watch with the cracked glass, a watch called TIMEX lying among the folds of a torn dress in the bins outside number 213. He'd kept it, brought it home, although clocks/watches were forbidden in the house.

(?why the watch?)

The watch. It was his SECRET. A secret like the other secret things he'd found: the magazine filled with pictures of men and women with no clothes on, the broken radio called HITACHI, the empty chocolate tin, the playing cards with naked ladies on them . . .

Blood pounded in his ears and his nose was running steadily now but he ignored the snot flowing over his lips as he rummaged in the drawer for the chocolate tin. He found it but couldn't open the lid because his fingers were slippery with sweat.

Open! Open!

The lid popped off.

There were the naked lady playing cards – and there was TIMEX. It was cold in his hand, yet reassuring in its simple, dangerous form. He put the torch down so he could wind it, wind it so the Crocodile would hear it. The stiff fingers of his left hand held TIMEX carefully as he fumbled with the tiny knob, slipped, turned harder. Once, twice, three times, four times.

Nothing.

TIMEX was ded.

He shook it.

Shook it again.

Then –

Tick, tick, tick . . .

The house was silent. It was out there though, oh yes, it was out there.

'I am a FREE MAN.'

He opened his mouth, placing TIMEX on his tongue.

Why the watch?

Because . . . because if you wanted to gain the power of your enemy you ate its heart to make you invincible and the Crocodile's heart was the clock that ticked ticked ticked inside it.

(national geographic)

The tribe called CA-NNIBALS ate the hearts of their enemies to take their strength. He knew. He'd read it in that magazine with the naked black women – *National Geographic* – yes, that was it. CA-NNIBALS ate their enemies and became as strong as them. CA-NNIBALS didn't eat CA-NNIBALS.

TIMEX was cold and didn't taste very nice. He hesitated, then swallowed.

And gagged.

TIMEX was in his throat. He tried to swallow again. It wouldn't move! He tried again.

Tick, tick, tick . . .

And started coughing.

Tick, tick, tick . . .

He couldn't breathe!

Tick, tick, tick . . .

He clawed at his throat. It felt like he had swallowed a rock. He gasped, fingernails gouging his skin. Gasping, gasping.

Tick, tick, tick . . .

No! No! It had tricked him. The Crocodile knew about TIMEX, had fooled him.

He felt faint as he tried to stand, still grasping his throat, retching, gasping. He stepped back putting his foot on the slick pages of a magazine. And fell over.

Tick, tick, tick . . .

He could hear it, hear the Crocodile coming.

Tick, tick, tick . . .

It was outside the door. He wheezed, trying desperately to breathe, fingers digging into his skin now. He had to –

Tick, tick, tick . . .

hehadto –

The Crocodile.
Tick, tick, tick. . . .
The Crocodi –
Tick, tick, ti –

The vanishing point

Brian Howell

Brian Howell was born in June 1961 in London. He studied German at Manchester University and became London film correspondent for Manchester's City Life *magazine, finding time also to write for* Films and Filming, Mancunion, Ms London, Ad Lib *and* TNT. *He wrote, directed and produced a 16mm rock promo and a two-minute film, in addition to which he has written four unoptioned screenplays.*

He has worked in various media-related positions such as managing the Camden Plaza and Everyman Cinema in London, and organising the IVCA Film and Video Festival. A short stint in the mail-order department of a large bookshop was followed by the delights of proofreading magazine ads. He escaped to Hungary and now teaches English in Budapest, when he's not working on his first novel and more scripts and short stories.

I first met Brian Howell at a press show of Andrei Tarkovsky's Nostalgia *– in retrospect a sad occasion as the great Russian director, who was present, didn't have long to live – but Brian claims to have no recollection of even attending that particular screening. We met at some other press show, he reckons, but doesn't know which.*

An interest in Dutch genre painting and a distinctive way of looking at the world inform The Vanishing Point, *which is Brian Howell's first published short story.*

The vanishing point

Dance could not recall exactly when the feeling of *being elsewhere* descended on him for the first time, except it somehow coincided with a series of odd incidents that would not normally cause him the slightest tinge of worry. He could not be quite sure whether the job he did was finally getting to him because of its unremitting routine or because he realized there were actually some aspects of it he did with relish but which he knew would ultimately lead nowhere.

These thoughts occupied him as the lift, that was to take him to the mail-order department on the fourth floor above the bookshop where he worked, stalled obstinately on the ground floor. The lift, it seemed to him, was a metaphor for what he was doing in this building, day in, day out – a metal cage going nowhere which would one day stall in the sweltering well of the building, only finally to spew him out into a limbo, shrivelled, desiccated, used up, yet unused. As the lift ascended, he tried to imagine it descending. It was a mental game he had started playing recently. The only thing to which it was akin in his experience was a realization he had once had as a child that it was impossible to fantasize everyday scenes in his head – where everything was based around vertical lines, as in a film – if he were in a horizontal position and still conscious of it. People had to be upright.

As he walked into the office, it might as well have been a desert, such was the sense of emptiness that suddenly came over him. Most of the time it seemed that he could only get through the day by dividing it artificially into twenty-minute or half-hour sections, with usually a coffee, tea, personal phone call, or trip to the toilet to separate the yawning expanses in between. There were, admittedly, some interesting aspects to the work, such as scanning the daily avalanche of mail from all corners of the country and globe. Strangely, the correspondence from the more eccentric customers gave him the most pleasure, as they at least appreciated his searching for some probably invented title or providing them with a list of books on famous deceased cats.

The morning frustrated Dance even more than usual, though he didn't trust himself to give too much thought to what 'usual' exactly was: a telephone order from an irate diplomat, who wanted the only existing English translation of de Sade's *Justine* – a trashy American one, Dance almost pointed out, but he didn't want to get drawn into a discussion on this topic in the office – before the diplomat left for Prague; an author of a famed and much reviled tome on blood sports rang to request that his book be sent to his grandchild for his eleventh birthday; and another outraged customer, from Wimbledon, wrote to reprimand him for having the audacity to address her by her first name – Daphne, in this case.

After running around the art department like a headless chicken for a good twenty minutes for an American calling from New York, Dance was suddenly taken by the urge to spend his whole lunch hour in the peace of the National Gallery, only a blessed five minutes away. He was glad he was allowed to take his lunch hour at the earliest possible moment, usually twelve o'clock. He had been reminded momentarily of the last time he'd felt like going to such trouble, when he had looked for a book on Dutch painting of which nobody in the department had heard. He had found it and sent it to a profusely grateful Miss

Groenehaven in Amsterdam, his favourite customer. He could no longer remember the title.

As ever, Dance strolled through the Italian Renaissance rooms, almost oblivious to the fact that he was in the Gallery (only the Titians raised a glimmer of interest), until he reached the Early Northern rooms where, as ever, he stopped in front of Holbein's *The Ambassadors*. Though the trick that Holbein was playing with an object in the foreground of the picture – a skull that could only be recognized if the viewer crouched down in the extreme lower left-hand corner, which otherwise looked like a shapeless blotch in front of the two illustrious Frenchmen – had long since lost its original fascination for Dance, he nevertheless always stopped to look at it – from the correct angle, on principle.

Finally, he reached the first of a series of rooms that contained for him all that he could wish for to keep him occupied, especially as an escape from a sour mood. He started off in the smallest room that contained the Dutch genre painters. The warden by the doorway smiled briefly in recognition of yet another visit by this young gangly man with the pale skin. Dance smiled back, then went on to circle the room, stopping for a while at a painting that depicted the remains of the municipal arsenal that had exploded in Delft in 1654 causing fires and deaths, including that of Carel Fabritius, a painter who had experimented with optical effects, as in his wide-angle *View in Delft* in another room. As Dance passed into the next room, he became aware of a high-pitched squeaking, an almost dog-like sound coming from somewhere outside the room he was in, which, if there had existed such an expression, he would have referred to as *déjà entendu*. He knew he had heard this sound before, but had forgotten about it until now. Would he forget this time too? Going back into the previous room he realized he could hear the sound there as well. Was he getting tinnitus? A friend had described the illness. Dance scolded himself for being paranoid; he was oversensitive about his eye-sight and hearing, forever afraid of losing the one or the other.

After pondering awhile over the sublime Hendrickje Stoffels, Rembrandt's companion and common-law wife till his dying days, Dance reached his favourite room that contained Vermeer, de Hooch, Metsu, Ter Borch, Fabritius, and many others. Dance was forever trying to work out what was going on in these scenarios, so often implying illicit liaisons and assignations. Reluctantly, Dance looked at his watch, knowing that he would have to dash back. What he saw at first filled him with a sense of relief, only to be almost immediately supplanted by one of terror. It was only 12.07, the exact time he had arrived at the Gallery almost an hour ago. Either his watch had stopped the moment he had arrived in the Gallery or he had left for lunch an hour early (surely he would have been given a few odd looks, going out with his satchel and jacket?).

He had stopped at a painting he had not seen before. The painter was anonymous, but the scene both totally familiar and yet intriguing. A young man and woman are seated either side of a table covered by an Ottoman carpet on which lies a book of sheet music. He is playing a theorbo and she a lute. Standing behind them is the music teacher, a gentleman of noble appearance in his early fifties. On the table are a flask and three glasses of wine. As the man turns the page, an unmistakable look passes between him and the woman, to which the teacher is oblivious, so much is he concentrating on the woman's playing. The three figures occupy the centre of the painting, whilst a tapestry is hung over the back wall. A dog sits by the edge of the tapestry next to the door. The foreground is dominated by a grid of floor tiles which obviously extend beyond the plane of the picture.

The way Dance viewed the painting, the closer the tiles came, the more distorted they seemed, as if shot through a wide-angle lens. This effect was heightened by the two bays of windows to the left of the room, whose receding lines contributed to the claustrophobia of the painting's background. Almost unconsciously, Dance fell into his usual habit of positioning himself as near to the artist's original position as possible. He had read that in certain cases, where the artist had used a *camera obscura* – a dark room with a peep-hole and lens – it was possible to calculate the exact position of the artist's eye. The image, it seemed, would be thrown through the hole, inverted, onto the back wall of the dark room, where the artist would trace over it. Dance decided to return to the Gallery at the next possible opportunity, but it couldn't be tonight as he'd arranged to play tennis with Matthew.

Back at work, after a few disapproving looks from his colleagues at his tardiness (mercifully, Banks, the supervisor, was out of the office, so he couldn't know how late Dance had been), Dance remembered his watch. He barely took in the fact that it said 1.13. How could it be? Was his watch having its own lunch break nowadays, resuming work only when its master decided to? He must have had a temporary lapse. He'd imagined it was 12.07 when it was 1.07. It was true he was prone to temporary lapses of perception or interpretation, but this had never been a serious problem, more a source of amusement for his friends. He laughed inwardly when he remembered how a few days earlier, whilst crossing the zebra to go into Sloane Square Underground station, he had prematurely drawn out his travel pass and waved it at the car waiting for him to go across. Fortunately, the driver had either not noticed this bizarre action or was too dumbfounded to react.

Dance's mind was soon ambushed by the usual spate of after-lunch telephone queries. The first was indeed a shock. It was Kim. Where had he been? Hadn't they arranged to meet at lunchtime? It was true. Dance had completely forgotten. He made a series of feeble excuses, only for her to hang up on him. The explanation would just have to wait until later tonight.

Dance's resulting bad mood was only relieved when Miss

Groenehaven rang from Amsterdam. After the niceties were over he told her about his most recent discovery in the Gallery. He knew Miss Groenehaven liked to be kept informed about any recent developments, as she came regularly to London. Dance knew nothing about her, except that she specialised in translating from English into Dutch, mainly art books, and that her father had recently died. She must be about thirty-five, he guessed from her voice, a deep voice that had a husky flavour to it so pleasurable that Dance invariably found himself not concentrating on what order he was writing down for her, so that he always had to ask her to repeat it. Dance harboured the desire one day to meet Miss Groenehaven, but could not as yet think of a way of indicating this without embarrassment. It was true he could not know for sure what she was like as a person, whether she was attractive in the flesh, but he was forever fascinated by the possibility that a certain compatibility between people who found each other attractive could be intuited, even across a distance such as this. To Dance it was a question of alignment, the formation of a regular pattern through a seemingly arbitrary agglomeration of components.

Miraculously, at mention of this new enigmatic picture in the Gallery, Miss Groenehaven informed Dance that she was coming to London for the weekend on Friday, in two days' time, and would make a point of searching it out. Would she like him to set the books aside so that she could call in and pick them up? Dance felt his heart leap when she acquiesced to his offer.

Now he had no need to make a clumsy invitation to her on the phone to go to the Gallery with him. He would meet her in person, then find some way of contriving a mutual visit. His only problem now was finding a way of getting off work on Friday to go with her. The best solution he could think of was to come in early and take a long lunch hour when he knew she would be going there. That would surely be OK with Banks.

* * *

As he approached the tennis court that evening Dance observed, as if for the first time, that the road that stretched out in front of him was only a road because its definition depended on the knowledge that without the phenomenon of receding perspective it would not be a road. Similarly, he mused, the brown poles, whose wires stretched from their tips to the tops of the houses at regular intervals, seemed more like they were supporting the houses from falling down rather than conveying telegraphic signals. The whole thing reminded him of a joke he had heard about an alien, who, coming to earth for the first time and knowing of human life solely from what he had seen on TV, walked into an art gallery to see everyone staring at these motionless frames on the walls. Why, he had nudged a pensive visitor to the gallery, don't they move? What is everyone staring at?

The game followed the usual pattern. Dance won the first set, went into a 4-0 lead in the second, only then to be pulled slowly into a game of attrition as his lead was eroded and pared down until he was behind 6-7, with Matthew serving. Matthew's initial sullen brooding had now been exchanged for a euphoric celebratory smirk. It was true that it was hard to tell exactly what his partner's facial expression was, hiding as he always did behind dark glasses.

Dance now started to hit the ball as if his life depended on every stroke. His concentration was momentarily disturbed when, running for a ball that Matthew had expertly hit straight down the far line, Dance's attention was arrested by a mass of golden fire descending on the periphery of his vision. He let the ball go, and stared at the apocalyptic sight. The fiery object now turned, and as it did so, the shining nose of a passenger plane identified itself, whilst the rest of the plane's body came into focus. Dance had simply seen the sun's reflection on the plane as it turned.

This momentary disturbance had cost Dance the set, but he was relieved nevertheless. He promptly went on to lose the next set and the match, mainly, he reasoned, due to his expectant thoughts of Miss Groenehaven's coming, but also to a recurring sensation that every time he went to connect with a returning ball, it was not he who was rushing to the ball, but rather the ball drawing his racket like a magnet to it. Dance imagined that even before he had stepped onto the court, a complex pattern of trajectories was already intricately mapped out. It was as though he were playing the game in reverse, starting from the last point, but thinking all the time he was proceeding from the beginning to the end.

When he got home and tried to ring Kim, her number was engaged all night. It didn't surprise him; she'd almost certainly taken the phone off the hook as a statement that she was not amused at his lunchtime lapse.

There was at least something to look forward to the next morning when he got into work – chasing up Miss Groenehaven's order. In fact, when he'd taken it he hadn't even given much thought to whether the books were stock items or not. He prayed that at least one of them was, so that he would be guaranteed being able to pass on one of the books. As it turned out, one of them was a standard work on Dutch genre painting which had just been re-edited. It was in the shop. The other was more of a curiosity, and a challenge – a theoretical work on perspective by a Dutch painter, Antonius Groenehaven. Groenehaven? How could that be? Surely, smitten as he was by Miss Groenehaven's voice, he had written down her name instead of the one he'd been meant to?

He tried the art department for anything by either a Groenehaven or an Antonius. Again, just a series of funny looks. In the office he checked all the possible directories, even out-of-print books, but could find no mention of this artist. Dance spent most of the day phoning every possible bookshop and institution to establish whether this book was in existence – to the detriment of other work, which piled up unceasingly. After a while Dance's obsession with this one book started to attract some attention, so he broke up his search for it to continue with other tasks.

Lunchtime seemed to arrive faster than ever before. Without really being conscious of it, Dance gravitated back to the National Gallery, where he stood before the painting, which might have been called *The Music Lesson*, but which was in fact named *The Duet*. Dance had been gazing at it for a good two or three minutes before he noticed something he hadn't seen the previous day. By the foot of the woman's shoe, which was propped up on a little wooden box, was a book. The only writing on the cover was in the lower right-hand corner – the signature, 'A. G.', in monogram, the 'G' forming a loop with the side of the 'A'.

Dance scanned the conflicting and converging eyelines of the three characters. Was the teacher's attention on the modest brow of the woman or, as now seemed possible, on the book, dropped by mistake – or on purpose – by one of the men or even the woman herself? Who was 'A. G.'?

Dance suddenly became aware of the squeaking sound he had previously heard, which now seemed to be accompanied by the gentle strains of a guitar melody. He looked round, stupidly expecting to find the source of the sound, which almost immediately ceased. Turning back to the painting and adopting his previous position in front of the canvas, he heard a laugh, more precisely a giggle, but he knew there was only a warden and an elderly man in the room at that moment. He tried to concentrate on the painting again, occasionally adjusting his position until he was as near to the artist's probable original position as possible. Instinctively, Dance glanced at his watch: 12.07. He could hardly believe his eyes. He decided to ask the warden. It was one o'clock. Once more, he would have to hurry back, destined to receive a barrage of disapproving looks.

One thought only kept Dance going through the afternoon, that of going back to the Gallery to gaze at that painting. Afterwards there would still be time to scour the secondhand bookshops around Charing Cross Road, which were usually open until eight o'clock in the evening. He knew it was an almost futile exercise, but he felt he had to try looking. Besides, if a book was out of print, what other way was there of obtaining it, besides advertising – for which it was too late? Otherwise, he could not face Miss Groenehaven and say he'd honestly looked everywhere.

Walking through the Gallery again Dance seemed to become aware of the same melody he had heard before, only this time it became louder the closer he got to the painting. Then it occurred to him. This sound he was hearing was not so much that of a guitar, as that of a lute. Approaching the picture, Dance suddenly felt dizzy as he observed another detail he was certain had not been there before. A hand, a man's hand, was gently pushing aside the tapestry at the back of the room. Dance felt inexplicably party to a drama that was unfolding for his sole attention – or entertainment. He looked around the room to see a young couple, arms entwined, lazily passing by the other paintings, enwrapped in some personal dispute that surely had nothing to do with any of the paintings. At one point Dance almost shushed them to be quiet and not to disturb the music, but checked himself just in time.

Dance looked at his watch. The Gallery would surely be closing in a few minutes. He was not certain if he had secretly wished it and unconsciously rejected it in the same thought, but his momentary fear and elation were confirmed when the time on his watch read 5.07. But he would have to check. Dance felt he was suffocating as he turned to the couple still lingering in the room. 'Hello . . . Sorry. Do you have the time? My watch . . .' They didn't hear him, couldn't. He tried again. Nothing. Then the warden. *They couldn't see him.*

Dance rushed out of the room into the next. It was empty, even of a warden. He went into the one after that. In this room stood an old woman studying a painting by Bosch, *Christ Mocked*. In desperation, Dance went up to the woman, grabbing her by the shoulder to reassure

himself that he hadn't been turned into a ghost as he darted
a garbled question at her. The old woman was so surprised
at the sudden attack that she let out a startled scream,
and fell fainting to the floor, where her face assumed an
expression of strange religious pathos that almost rivalled
that of Bosch's Christ. Dance recoiled, relieved that he
was still in the land of flesh and blood, but worried that
his action might be interpreted as some kind of assault.
He moved so quickly through the Gallery that he could
not be sure whether anyone had witnessed his strange
behaviour.

Outside, he took a deep breath, coaxed into a state of
calmness by the familiar sight of Trafalgar Square, pinned
down as it was by the weight of the Column, given its
movable contours by the steady stream of red buses.
Despite the relief of seeing this great open space, Dance
moved almost like a blind man up the curve of Charing
Cross Road till it evened out at Leicester Square and the
line of bookshops began along one side of the street. In
his panic Dance had forgotten about his resolve to look
for Miss Groenehaven's book, but now saw the beckoning
shops as a refuge from his immediate worries.

In the basement of one secondhand shop, Dance found
a section on art divided helpfully into countries. He was
impressed by this judicious system, as it was all too
common (he knew from collecting hardback fiction) to
find slung together books which rightfully belonged to
different categories without even an attempt at putting
them in alphabetical order. It was the more unusual as this
was the reserve collection, the main one being upstairs.

Mechanically, he thumbed the index of every book that
might have even the most tentative relevance to Dutch
genre painters. Dance had checked every book, except
those on the top shelf, which he had left till last, as
staring up at high shelves always blurred his vision and
gave him a headache. Using a small stepladder, he could
just scan the top shelf without straining too much. It was
the last book of all that confirmed Dance's intuition, as

he lifted out an 1870 English edition of *On the Theory of Perspective* by one Antonius Groenehaven. So it was true! But it surely didn't prove anything. After all, if there were any connection between his Miss Groenehaven and this Antonius Groenehaven, she would have mentioned it. It was probably quite a common name.

Nevertheless, Dance was so exhilarated by his find that he nearly toppled off the ladder. It wasn't until he reached the cash desk that he thought of looking for the price of the book – £20.00! He searched frantically in his wallet, knowing that he had drawn out £30.00 the day before, but not daring to calculate how much of it he might have already spent. His wallet contained £21.50, leaving just enough to buy a little food for the evening.

Dance had already ploughed through the first twenty pages of the book on the journey home by tube, though he knew he would have to re-read them later; even with the most gripping thriller he usually had to return to the beginning when he'd finished. His initial excitement at an impending good read – fiction or not – inevitably impaired his concentration and ability to absorb some essential fact or other. To his dismay, the text was dense with allusions and generalities that did not seem to touch on the immediate subject matter, and the prose convoluted. Nevertheless, Dance steeled himself against bouts of sleepiness to have a reasonable chance of finishing the book by the early hours of the morning. He could not bear the possibility of being tongue-tied in front of Miss Groenehaven when she called in the next day. When Kim rang, a conciliatory note evident in her voice after the temporary lapse in their relations, Dance had to refuse her invitation to go over to her place. His weak excuse that he'd arranged to see a friend only served to reawaken her present penchant for recriminations.

By three o'clock in the morning Dance had finally finished the book, having kept himself awake with a combination of coffee and short bursts of watching television.

Tired as he was, Dance imposed on himself the discipline of making a résumé of what Groenehaven's book was about. He came to the conclusion that the author – who was obviously an artist of some repute, although he kept references to his own works to a modest minimum – held the view that the best paintings of his time were those that through the exact mathematical calculation of perspective drew the viewer out of himself into another world whilst giving him a total sense of being a witness to the ordinary and everyday. To this effect the tract became no more nor less than a defence of the artist's use of the *camera obscura*, forerunner of the camera.

There was, however, another concern to this treatise, away from a full elaboration of which the author seemed to shy. Groenehaven's view was that an ideal position existed which the viewer could adopt to put himself exactly in that of the original artist. Locating it depended on finding a number of clues that existed in the paintings themselves. The most crucial of these was the vanishing point, the point at which the receding lines that gave the illusion of space – such as the skirting board or the horizontal frames of a window – would converge, if extrapolated. This point indicated the exact height of the artist's eye. Unfortunately, the author did not go into any details about how to adopt this position, leaving the reader tantalisingly to conclude that he would have to stumble upon it by chance.

Dance finally fell into a fitful sleep, his mind so exhausted that it was working overtime on fantasies of what it was like to fall asleep. Somewhere between his conscious imaginings and occasional moments of selfless flight, Dance saw a woman of about twenty-five in a satin dress, her hair tied back in a bun, enter his room. She smiled at him, then moved towards the curtained window. Gesturing as if to indicate something remarkable was in store, she pulled aside the curtains, first one side, then the other. Instead of the expected darkness Dance now saw, as if through the frame of the anonymous painting in the Gallery, the gentleman with the theorbo held loosely in his hand, and the teacher pacing about the room with a pained expression while the woman's lute lay in the foreground. The teacher and the man were evidently having an altercation of some kind while waiting for the woman to join them. Eventually, the woman appeared from behind the tapestry on the wall, but it was impossible in the dimness to see what was behind it. The woman demurely took up her lute and the duet commenced.

It was only the grinding chords of a song on the radio in the flat downstairs that drew Dance out of his deep slumber. He was terrified to see it was already 8.30. In his exhausted stupor he had obviously forgotten to set his alarm – today of all days!

As the train thundered out of the tunnel along the platform at Finsbury Park, Dance noticed how it gripped the lines that got ever wider the closer it came to him, filling out the space that at the other end had seemed so much smaller. He got into work at 9.15. Mercifully, nobody said anything.

Almost his first action was to check with the call desk to make absolutely sure that Miss Groenehaven would be sent up to see him if by mistake she was directed to the place people usually picked up books. After that the morning dragged more slowly than ever before. Dance's intake of coffee had reached new levels of excess, necessitating an irritating frequency to relieve himself in the gents' one floor below.

On one such visit, as he stared blankly out of the toilet window studying the workmen doing their balancing acts on the scaffolding, hoping they would not notice him (it was too hot to shut the window), Dance switched his attention to the converging grey tiles on the wall. Irresistibly, he found himself pulled towards the tiles, looking along their length and following the orthogonal lines to the wall. Feeling that he had to do justice to their construction, he stepped to the back of the toilet, and became aware of the lines where the walls and ceiling met. Following these lines, he tried to imagine them going beyond the window and continuing into space. A strange sense of serenity came over him. Looking down at the floor, however, he was shocked to notice how badly fitted were the black and white linoleum tiles, which in some places proceeded at acute angles into the walls, instead of running alongside them. Cursing his reluctant bladder and whoever had fitted the tiles, Dance felt an overwhelming sensation of dizziness descend on him. He pulled himself together when he remembered that he needed to be in the office all the time for Miss Groenehaven.

The morning and afternoon progressed without any sign of his visitor. Dance's lunch hour was on hold. It occurred to him that just possibly Miss Groenehaven had decided to go and see the painting before she picked up her books. He stayed till just before 5.30, and rushed to the room in the Gallery, the Groenehaven book in his hand, keeping his face lowered and turned away from any warden who might recognize him from the day before. In the room where his painting hung there was only one woman, her back turned away from him, surveying the painting in detail. Dance realized that this was the first time he had noticed anyone besides himself actually paying attention to *The Duet*.

He sensed that the woman, whose face he could only see in profile, was occupying the coveted position so mysteriously hinted at by Groenehaven's theory. Dance noticed the figure's almost imperceptible movements as she slightly adjusted her position, her gaze following the lines made by the two bays of windows.

Dance, becoming ever more anxious that Miss Groenehaven would make a last-minute entry, only for their view to be permanently hogged by this woman, started to circle her from behind at a polite distance.

To Dance's surprise, she turned round and looked at

him directly. Dance's reaction was somewhere between
fear and wonderment as he recognized the woman from
his dream adopting the same gesture and smiling as she
had done previously when drawing aside the curtain of
his window to reveal this same scene, slightly altered, of
the lute player, the theorbo player, and the teacher. He
hadn't expected any words. He had almost expected the
same scene to unfold as in the dream.

This woman now looked directly at Dance. He was too
shocked to say anything. Then, startlingly, the woman
took his hand. Her hand was ice-cold, but the rest of
her body and particularly her face radiated a heat strong
enough to make him feel sweat trickling down his back.
Without saying anything, she made him stand beside her
as they scrutinized the painting.

'I knew you would come. You have the book.' The
voice was unmistakable. It was Miss Groenehaven. Dance
craned his neck to study her features more closely. She
could have been the twin modern-day sister of the woman
in the painting.

'Yes, here,' Dance stated proudly, not quite believing
his ears and eyes as he held out Groenehaven's work.
He felt the woman brace herself as she took the volume,
placing her hands over his, only reluctantly letting him slip
them out.

She stepped aside slightly to let Dance stand in the
correct position. 'My father wrote the treatise. There
was only ever one copy in his lifetime – it was stolen,
translated, and sold abroad. My father was a broken
man with impending incarceration for old debts his only
immediate prospect, when Hendrick, the fiancé that you
see playing the theorbo, finally had the courage to offer
his hand and wealth.'

She moved closer to Dance, gripping his hand intensely.

'Look at your watch.'

It was 5.35. Again, no time had passed since he
had entered the Gallery. Dance looked into her eyes
beseechingly.

She looked back at the painting. 'Can you see what is happening?'

He was about to venture an interpretation, but he was cut off by Miss Groenehaven's almost confessional need to elucidate the painting's content.

'The figure of the teacher is a self-portrait, the painting a wedding gift, sorely resented by my husband, such was his interpretation of the inclusion of the all-too-familiar book by my foot. He tried to destroy the painting. Finally, I persuaded him to sell it anonymously, so that my father's memory would survive, albeit in uncertain and unknown hands.

'Despite his handsome looks and the promise of his various industrious enterprises, Hendrick's life ended in dissolution and sadness. He seemed forever haunted by worries and preoccupations to which he could never give proper expression. I never told him of my father's suspicion that it was indeed Hendrick who had stolen the treatise, and never believed it myself until I discovered this lost painting after Hendrick's death. Perhaps as some kind of expiation, Hendrick told me on his deathbed where he had hidden the painting. As I studied it over the years I realized my father had painted this picture as a testimony. The book on the floor by my foot, as you can see, carries his well-known signature, 'A.G.'

'Antonius Groenehaven,' murmured Dance.

A certain hardness of expression in Miss Groenehaven's face was now replaced by a flush of animation as she gripped hold of Dance's wrists.

'I have been waiting so long to reclaim my father's reputation. Now, with your help . . .'

She beckoned once more to the painting.

The words came out before his realization.

'The hand . . .'

'Behind the tapestry is a coat-stand, where my husband-to-be would hang his coat. In a few minutes, when the duet has ended, he will get up and collect his coat . . . At this time we still could no longer afford servants.'

'You want me to murder him?'

'You would be doing humanity and science a favour. With the book reclaimed and our knowledge of how things work now . . .'

Dance thought of the book once more, the potential for applying Groenehaven's theories with hindsight, of meeting the great masters in person, of Miss Groenehaven . . . Groenehaven, perhaps wisely, had not chosen to make public the full extent of his discovery. Dance imagined how history could be changed with the proper application of such knowledge. For, if it was possible to go back now to an earlier time, it was surely possible to go forward from that time, not just to now, but maybe even the future. Dance had often wondered how life would have progressed if motion pictures had existed before the turn of the nineteenth century.

He looked at Miss Groenehaven. He could not allow her to go through such a life again.

Imperceptibly, the sound of a harpsichord reached his ears, whilst the light in the room dimmed to near darkness, then it was pitch dark.

Dance realized Miss Groenehaven had disappeared. He moved around the room. It had become much cooler. Dance felt as if his body were adapting to another atmosphere or climate.

The sound of the harpsichord coming from a distant room was interrupted by that of a knock on a door. A dog gave a welcoming whine as people entered the room. Dance felt in front of him a heavy cloth, which he pushed aside by minute degrees until he could see the interior of the room that was now so very familiar; the gentleman from the painting, taking up his theorbo, an easel placed five or six feet from the scene, Groenehaven himself, and, at the opposite end of the room the lens hole of Antonius Groenehaven's *camera obscura*. Groenehaven kissed his daughter on the cheek, and as he entered his dark room the couple began to play. Miss Groenehaven cast a glance across the room as she noticed the protruding hand, perhaps by way of warning, perhaps by way of signalling her assent.

Common land

Joel Lane

Joel Lane was born in Exeter in 1963. Brought up in Birmingham, he went to Cambridge to study history and philosophy of science, then returned to Birmingham where he now lives and works as a journalist. His stories, poems and critical articles have appeared in various magazines and anthologies including Panurge, Fantasy Tales, Dark Dreams, Skeleton Crew, Dark Horizons, Ambit, Critical Quarterly, Winter Chills. *Two stories –* The Foggy, Foggy Dew *and* The Earth Wire – *have been reprinted in* The Year's Best Horror Stories (*volumes XV and XVIII*). *His interests/influences include social theory, rock/folk music, ghost stories and the urban environment.*

There must be something about Birmingham. Just as in London, where horror writers gather around Crouch End like bees around a honeypot (or flies around a body), Birmingham attracts more than its fair share of writers of the macabre. Joel Lane, Chris Morgan, Pauline Dungate, Dave Sutton and Jovan Panich live on adjoining pages of the A-Z. In Common Land *Joel Lane draws upon the decaying landscape of the inner city – specifically Birmingham as in* The Foggy, Foggy Dew – *but the symptoms of blight as he describes them are by no means peculiar to the Midlands. He brings these urban darklands to life. But it's a twisted, horrifying kind of a life, owing more to* Eraserhead *than* Genesis.

Common Land is Joel Lane's first sale to an original horror anthology. In his own words, it is 'a story about the betrayal of ideals'.

Common land

She went to New Street Station to meet him. Stephen's letter had been forwarded from her old address, and he wouldn't know where to look for her. Rosalind waited outside the ticket barrier, in a brightly lit underground hall that, late at night, was filled with silent people. Some were waiting for trains, others for people walking through from the street; and others would stand until they were moved on. In his letter, Stephen had said he was homeless now. Rosalind wondered just what that meant. But the letter had a local postmark; why had he made her come here, when he could have met her in town during the day? She supposed it was one of his gestures, intended to make her feel something. Just after eleven, Rosalind thought she saw Stephen waving goodbye to someone on the far side of the ticket barrier. He came through alone, carrying a weekend bag and wearing a green overcoat that she'd not seen before, though it looked old.

He was pleased to see her. 'I didn't know if you'd be free. I've got a lot to tell you.' They walked up through the shopping arcades to the New Street ramp. Stephen was visibly tired, though he seemed inwardly worked up about something. His eyes flickered briefly at everyone who passed by. Rosalind didn't know what to ask him. Besides, she realised, the silence that had brought them face to face again might be broken by discussion. They were in time for the last bus to Northfield. The city centre seemed full of young couples, embracing in the bus shelters and shop doorways. The rain whitewashed the pavements.

Rosalind's flat – strictly speaking, a bedsit with its own sink and electric cooker – was part of one of the large houses on the main road. There was no light on the staircase. Stephen followed her up to the second floor. Inside, he stared around him as though displaced. The room was fairly chaotic; half of it was taken up by the table, on which she'd placed a large square of hardboard. This was now covered with newspaper and twisted hulks of red clay, parts of which glistened like poor special effects. Stephen sat on the couch and wrapped his arms across his chest. The stubble on his cheeks only showed up how pale his skin was. Rosalind lit the gas fire, though it was only September and she didn't feel cold herself.

'Do you remember our first year?' he said. He meant the first year at art college, when the two of them had lived in a house with three other students. They hadn't been going out together then. 'I'm trying to get another group together, like that. A commune, really. I'd like you to meet them.' He hesitated, and glanced across at the table. 'What are you doing now? Selling your work?'

'Trying to. I'm on an enterprise allowance.' They both laughed at that. Among the rough figures drying on the hardboard were a child's head with pale blue marbles for eyes and a human foot with wings growing from either side of the Achilles tendon. 'From now until next June, I'll be trying to make and sell things like these.'

'That's good. I've not done anything like that since leaving college. Actually I've been travelling around. Meeting different kinds of people.' He talked slowly, letting gaps form between his words and what he meant to say. Rosalind was just glad that he was back. Behind where he was sitting, though he hadn't noticed it, there was a painting which he'd done of her the year before last. It caught her in a rather stiff posture, closed in by an

146

abstract grey background. She was half turned away, her features sharply defined and detailed, eyes shut. Rosalind had used to think the painting proof of Stephen's feelings for her.

'I'm not working,' he went on. 'Not officially, anyway. There's a group of us, we're moving into an empty house in Deritend, this week. It's not easy. You'll have to see for yourself, the way we live. And what the point of it is. We use whatever we can find. Like gypsies. Self-help, I suppose you could call it. That's the way I was brought up.' Stephen had come from a deprived region, one of the enclosed towns of the Black Country that had a city's landscape and a village's culture. Rosalind had a comfortable suburban background, and the differences had always stuck between them. He fell into silence. The room was warm now, the steady firelight stamping a grid on Rosalind's eyes.

'We can talk in the morning,' she said. It was ridiculous for them to have said so little to each other; but she needed to sleep, not to think. They sat on the bed under the window at the far end of the room. Stephen muttered something, thanked her for going to meet him. She unbuttoned his shirt. He was thinner than she remembered. Her hand stopped just below his rib-cage, on the left side. There was something there that felt solid and cold under the skin, though the surface was unmarked. 'Does that hurt?' He shook his head. She pressed it, and thought of touching the half-frozen snow on a hedge. Her hands began to shake.

'Don't worry,' he said. 'There's nothing the matter.' He took her hands and pressed them together, then drew her head forward and kissed her, breathing into her throat. They made love very slowly and tenderly, hardly moving, as though it hurt them to draw apart. The night seemed to dissolve the building, pulling them down into each other. Rosalind felt lost; she was never at home in passion. At a rational level, she didn't believe that she had missed him this much. Stephen held her without forcing, almost

147

childlike in his need. The thread of joy stretched tighter in the darkness, then broke, letting them slip apart from each other and into sleep.

When Rosalind awoke, her first thought was that it had somehow become winter. Stephen's breath was misted above his face, like scratches on a window. He was lying on his side, facing her; his dark hair was stuck to his forehead. His eyelids were twitching, as though his dreams were struggling toward the light. As she watched, a series of white threads drifted from his mouth and joined the cloud that was forming there. It seemed about to assume some definite shape. Stephen's mouth opened wider, and a continuous stream of fibres linked it to the slowly hardening veil that now covered his face, becoming nearly opaque.

Shocked at herself, Rosalind reached up and touched the caul. It was soft as cotton, with harder fragments like seeds or crystals. The material did not tear, but the warmth of her hand dissolved it; soon there was nothing left. Stephen's face tensed, losing the gentleness of sleep; his eyes opened. They looked at each other. 'We need your help,' he said.

'We? You mean – '

'Me and the others.' He smiled. 'Or me and . . . whatever's inside. What did it look like? I mean, *who* did it look like?'

Rosalind hadn't asked herself that. 'I don't know. Not like anyone in particular. Have you seen . . .'

'It seems to take different shapes. From me, from other people. There are five of us. In the house.' He sat up, and began to dress. Rosalind held back; she was afraid to touch him, for various reasons. Stephen made no move towards her. 'There's nothing to explain,' he said. 'What we really need is some way to form. It's no good trying on your own. We need someone who can bring it together for us. Then we'll know what's going on.' He was very nervous; Rosalind knew that he was afraid she'd reject him. She knew what he was like. Stephen broke the deadlock by putting on his coat. He took a notebook from the inside pocket, wrote something down and tore out the page. 'That's where we're going to live,' he said. 'Come and visit us, if you want to. Soon.' He kissed her goodbye; his mouth tasted quite ordinary.

Over the next fortnight, Rosalind found a craft shop in Hagley and another in Evesham that would take her clay sculptures. She began working on a series of rather delicate masks, using paler clay and a brittle varnish that made her feel lightheaded and sickly. The week after that, she went to find Stephen's house. Deritend wasn't an area where a great many people lived – or at least, not one where many people had homes. It was a district in transition between the city centre and the suburbs. Nothing old there had remained intact, but nothing had been removed either. Parts of various buildings had been taken over by wholesalers or manufacturers, who had put new signboards over the ground-floor windows; while the upper storeys were left to decay, their elaborately carved roofs and window-frames stripped naked by the weather. Just off the High Street, a church had been turned into a warehouse for general works equipment; its roof now consisted of reinforced glass set in a lattice of wooden beams.

Even the A-Z map was an unreliable guide to the maze of backstreets, overlaid with railway bridges and new expressways. Series of identical terraced houses were juxtaposed with minor factories, car parks, derelict buildings, canals. Near where Stephen lived, the windows of a pub had been boarded over; someone had chalked WELCOME across one of the boards. Next to that, a scrap yard was full of cars piled three or four high and rusting steadily, like toys in the back of a cupboard. Rosalind walked under a bridge that crossed the main road, in the dip of a little valley. The sudden darkness and smell of rot made her pause and struggle to remember something. She felt displaced. The roof of the bridge was furred with black crystals. What looked like nails driven through it from above were in fact hollow pipes of lime sediment, formed by gradual seepage of water. A few of their tips glittered with an unexpected brightness, dripping.

Beyond the bridge, a line of houses faced the brick embankment of the railway. This was where the commune, Stephen and his friends, were staying. The house was thin and crusted with the same pollution as the bridge; but the windows and their net curtains were clean. There was a small front yard, where rose bushes and brambles were tangled together, obstructing the path. Rosalind knocked on the door. A middle-aged woman in a baggy green sweater opened it. 'Are you Rosalind?' she asked. Rosalind nodded, taken aback. 'Well then, come inside.' The interior of the house smelled of cooking and damp. Stephen and two younger men, who looked very like one another, were sitting in the kitchen. Stephen looked worse than he had the last time; he embraced her before speaking. Then he introduced her to the others. The woman's name was Sandra; she came from Leeds, and had been an actress. The two youths, Lee and Mike, were non-identical twins; they came from Glasgow. There was another tenant, a bearded silent man called Alan, whom Rosalind met later.

To begin with, Stephen was the only one that Rosalind had any real contact with. She came over to the house every few days, and slept with him; or sometimes he stayed over at her flat in Northfield. For Rosalind, it seemed like a chance to relive the early weeks of their relationship, now three years in the past. His illness, or whatever it was, had the effect of making him gentler and more dependent. She enjoyed taking care of him, and using the therapy to ease her own tensions and fears at the same time. He was a mirror for her, as she secretly knew and had always known. She assumed it would end, either when he recovered himself and got bored with her (as had happened before), or when she found a permanent job and moved away from the area.

If Rosalind got used to the strange material, it was only

because she didn't allow anything to do with Stephen to be quite real. That was her way of not getting too involved. The sight and touch of it fascinated her. She remembered having seen photographs of séances from the nineteenth century where the same effect was produced. Stephen needed to be asleep for it to happen. She watched him in the night, until something formed out of his throat and diffused above him. It was colder than flesh, and didn't respond to air currents. Once the tissue spread across the upper half of Stephen's body, like fresh bark on a silver birch tree. It cocooned him for hours. Rosalind thought he was dying; she lay there unable to move, until his skin was clear again.

Sometimes Rosalind thought of it as a living thing, a homeless being that had taken possession of Stephen and made him alien to her. Then she'd draw away from him, make him come to her and prove that she was needed. When they were close once more, she thought of the emissions as inert: a waste product, the traces of some unrecognisable industry. By day, she and Stephen worked together on her sculptures and pottery. They ate together, went for walks, saw films, sometimes made love. Stephen watched her all the time, obsessed as before with her image. In early December, when the frost and the shrunken daylight made travelling difficult, and she couldn't afford the heating costs of her flat, Rosalind moved in with the commune.

The others accepted her, without particularly trying to make her feel at home. Rosalind and Stephen shared one room; Lee and Mike shared another; while Sandra and Alan had their own rooms. It took Sandra more than a week to start talking to Rosalind, but after that she seemed to take to the newcomer in a maternal kind of way, proving an unexpected source of advice. Her conversation was a mixture of practicality and folklore. She told Rosalind a lot about her past: travelling, the theatre, cities and lovers. Much of it was inconsistent and probably made up. But Rosalind found it strangely reassuring to think that she, too, would eventually have a past. Something else that Sandra told her stuck in her mind: that you could get a man by making a clay effigy of one and wrapping it in coils of your own hair.

One evening, when Sandra had a cold and stayed in her room, Rosalind took her up a bowl of soup. She knocked on the door and heard the answer: 'Come in.' When she opened the door, she thought Sandra was lying under a sheet. At once, her mind registered the presence of the dead. 'It's all right,' Sandra said clearly; a whitish skein lifted from her and hung between the two women, losing itself as Rosalind's eyes focused in the half-light. She felt as though her own reflection had glanced off a window or a basin of water. She knelt beside Sandra's bed, feeling giddy, and put the bowl down. The smell of boiled onions twisted in her head. The older woman reached down and took her hands, saying 'It's all right. You're just not ready yet. Give it time.'

It wasn't until Rosalind had moved in that she realised one of the area's deficiencies. There were almost no telephone boxes. She had to walk nearly a mile toward the city centre to make a phone call. What the area did have was many public toilets, at least the small kind built into the alcoves of walls: uniform metal boxes with ornate designs on the panels. They were useless to women. By night, it was anybody's guess which buildings were derelict and which in use. Local business was a testament to the idea of self-help. That could mean opening bed and breakfast accommodation on the ground floor of an abandoned building, leaving the upper storeys empty and blackened with half a century's dirt. Or cutting the shell of a factory down to head level, making it an enclosed scrap yard. Or using a terraced house with barred windows as a small warehouse for building materials or the like. Houses and churches were just more kinds of wall.

The dead tissue that Stephen and the others breathed limited the commune. That was how Rosalind came to see it, without being able to explain the effect. The simplicity of their lives was partly chosen and partly involuntary. They were poor, but that wasn't it. They were like patients; life had closed in on them. They worked, on and off, in the local trades. Alan was a factory's night watchman. Sandra cooked and served in an all-night café. The twins helped to load and unload trucks for the salvage department. Stephen was probably the most idle of the group; his main occupation was being the leader of their peculiar rituals. The house wasn't very fit to live in. They kept the kitchen hygienic, but the damp and grime elsewhere couldn't be dealt with. A lot of their furniture came from local rubbish tips or empty houses. They had electricity, but expense and dangerously faulty wiring deterred them from using the power points. For warmth, they depended on paraffin heaters and clothing. Rosalind tried to believe that the end would justify the means.

If only so much weren't hidden from her. One night, when she went to the bathroom to relieve herself, the washbasin was furred up with strands of ectoplasm. She tore a piece of it away; it had the feel of numbness. She could just make out her hand behind it in the dark. Another time, Rosalind tried to call Stephen's bluff. 'Why do you want me here?' she said. 'I don't belong. Nothing happens when I'm around . . . What does it mean? It's that different I can't talk about it or think about it. I don't know how you can live here.' Stephen faced the window, staring at the blackened wall of the embankment, the arches bricked up. 'Speak to me. Tell me something.'

He turned round and looked at her, without changing his expression. Rosalind walked out of their bedroom and down the stairs to the front door. Stephen leaned over the banister in the hallway and appeared to blow her a kiss. Clouds trailed from his hand. She spent that night in the café, wrapped in her depression as though it were alcohol, watching all the homeless people come, stay and eventually go. They could make a cup of coffee or a cigarette last an hour and occupy them completely. They talked in rituals, giving bits of themselves that they were used to giving, holding onto familiar phrases. *Nearly morning. Where you been? Just one more.* If you said something unexpected, they wouldn't hear you.

Over Christmas, Rosalind went to stay with her father and stepmother in Stafford. They'd been living there for five years, and were gradually redecorating and refurnishing the house, so that every time she went back it was like somewhere different. She felt like a child again. What she couldn't mention seemed to get into every word she said and take away its impulse. Rather than sit in the living-room and watch TV, she walked around the town, which looked unreal in its coating of frost and sodium light. For some reason, the sound of carol-singers frightened her; not the songs, but the chorus of voices. On Christmas Eve they attended midnight mass at the cathedral. Rosalind kept thinking: *You haven't got me fooled, you two. Pretending to belong.* Her childhood hadn't been this peaceful, or this normal. It wasn't reality either.

I could tell you a few things about communion. Her last night with Stephen, she'd taken some of the plasma and tried to eat it. She'd stopped almost at once, because of the images it brought to mind. It tasted of nothing at all. She'd thought of cancer, the body eating itself. Or of primitive magic, someone eating nerves to make herself better able to feel.

Rosalind went back to the house near the end of December. In the thin daylight the countryside seemed pure and featureless, like a face that hid its age in sleep. Trees and hedges were sketched in charcoal. As the train came into Birmingham, the environment darkened. It was slightly warmer here; the veneer of frost gave way to a matt vapour. Factory chimneys bruised the clouds grey and yellow. She was thinking of Stephen. Perhaps she'd get him away from the others, soon, and the two of them could go to live somewhere in the country, say in Evesham. She wanted to hide in the privacy of their bedroom. Sculpt figures and make love with Stephen, and sleep through the long vacant nights. Everything seemed possible again.

She had to try several times before her key would turn in the lock. Evidently the cold had warped the doorframe. None of the windows were lit. As she stood cursing at the front door, a goods train shuddered along the embankment behind her. Eventually Rosalind got the door open; the hall was dark. She flicked the light switch. *Fucking hell*. Either the antique wiring had given out or they'd been disconnected. Or else it was a power cut. Some light came through the windows in the kitchen. All the commune were standing in there. Just standing together, quite close, facing inward. They must have heard her struggling with the door. But even now, they ignored her. She was so angry that at first she didn't notice what they were looking at.

It was rather like the stream of ashes in the heat-haze over a bonfire. But as Rosalind watched, it took on form, becoming a kind of effigy. This time, she knew it was using her eyes to define itself. Each member of the group standing round it was connected to it at the mouth, by a glistening thread of vapour. The plasma only shone where it caught the light. Rosalind couldn't identify the figure, no matter how intently she looked at it. It had a thin body, with arms folded over its breasts, and a wreath of long hair around its face. But the face itself was somehow impersonal. The features were empty. Rosalind had the impression that they were reversed, the eyes and mouth opening inward; though that was not what she saw. It made her think of an identikit face in a newspaper; though she had never seen a female one, and found it very hard to accept this image as a woman. She pressed herself against the wall, feeling powerless, and wrapped her arms around herself in an unconscious mimicry of the creature.

The others drew back, apparently sensing that they had done what they could. For the first time, Rosalind could see how tired they were, as if they had not slept since her departure. Sandra sat down at the kitchen table and

covered her face with her hands. Lee and Mike caught
hold of each other and stood motionless by the window.
Alan walked slowly through the doorway and up the stairs.
Stephen turned toward Rosalind, reached out and touched
her arm. 'Look after her,' he said. That was all he said. It
was Rosalind he was speaking to. The grey-white figure
settled itself on the floor, its arms around its knees; its
head dropped forward. It grew fainter and lost some of
its outline, but did not go away. It would not move for
several hours.

More out of fear than concern for the others, Rosalind
made herself do some housework. The sink was heaped
with plates and cups, none of which appeared to have
been used recently. She scrubbed a few clean and piled
the rest on the sideboard, not knowing when they'd have
some hot water. Probably the others needed a meal; she
certainly did, after the journey. The only food in the
larder was dried, and months old: rice, lentils, pasta shells.
There weren't even any tins. She went out to buy some
fresh food and milk. When she came back, nothing had
happened. She took the shirts and underclothes from the
clothes-horse at the foot of the stairs, folded them and
piled them up on a chair. They had dried hard, though
the air had touched them with damp. She cooked some
soup on the paraffin stove, though its fumes nearly made
her pass out.

Rosalind and Stephen ate, leaving a half-full pot on the
stove for the others. The cold thing of breath and threads
watched them from the floor, passively. When it grew
dark outside, since they had no light, they went up to
bed. Stephen fucked her twice, hard; her release was like
shedding a skin. They slept huddled under the blankets.
The next day they awoke after dawn; they clung together,
kissing and whispering, until it was dark once more. The
day after that, they got up. Rosalind washed herself and
pulled clothes onto a body that still felt unreal. All the
time, she knew she was being watched.

The life of the commune made more sense now. Every

day, all the others would gather round the maiden-creature and breathe matter into it. The rest of the time, they hardly spoke or gave attention to anything. Rosalind felt left out. What was expected of her was something different. She talked and acted for the maiden. She couldn't talk to it, but she talked to herself or Stephen, and the thing listened. Sometimes it followed her in the house, like a voiceless double. It mimicked her posture and the movements of her hands.

Rosalind could feel everything she did or said taking on a new intensity, like performance. She relived events from her childhood, making stories of them, weaving in lines from traditional songs that she hadn't realised she still knew. The blank-faced creature took in everything. It saw her and Stephen in bed together. It saw her panic on finding a nest of silverfish in the larder, then boil water to get rid of them, and then spill the water and scald herself badly. It saw her crying, swallowing painkillers, bleeding, coughing up phlegm from a cold on her chest. This went on for nearly a fortnight.

One morning, a few days into the new year, Rosalind walked out of the house. The sunlight dazzled her; she had to keep stopping until her head cleared. The upper windows of half-ruined buildings showed her the sky. From the doorway of the café where Sandra worked, a man whistled at her. 'Get the message, love.' She had a toothache. A yard full of silver-headed thistles was enclosed on three sides by blocks of flats, with washing hanging from the balconies. The harvest of seeds caught the light. A few hours later, when Rosalind was back in the house, she realised that she couldn't actually have seen that.

When Stephen saw she was ill, he told her: 'You'd better leave.' She ought to have known he wouldn't change. He spent more time close to the ghost-creature now, communing with it in a way she couldn't. She'd watched him kiss it, breathing substance into its blurred face. 'It's not enough,' he said. 'You have to give yourself.

You can't do it. It's not your fault.' Rosalind realised that he wasn't concerned about her at all.

'What more do you want?' They were standing in the bedroom. Rosalind's face twisted with bitter emotions until it felt like a mask. Even her sense of failure was probably being used – and she didn't know for what. It was all hidden. Stephen looked out of the window, again. He was unshaven; it gave him the appearance of strength. Rosalind seized his arms and kissed him fiercely, trying to claim him. He turned away as though nauseated, and stared at the glass.

'Nothing in particular,' he muttered. 'You're not the first. And you won't be the fucking last.'

Later that day, while Stephen was out of the house, Rosalind took out a half-full bottle of vodka that she kept among her clothes in a suitcase. She drank it all, mixed with water. A strange feeling of indifference grew in her. It felt like a snow child lodged in her abdomen. She collected together whatever tablets she could find – codeine, paracetamol, a dozen or so sleeping pills prescribed a long time back. She swallowed them all, sitting on the edge of the bath, watching the water run from the tap like a stream of pure light. It took more than an hour. Finally she went back into the bedroom, drew the curtains, and lay down on the bed.

She woke up in the night, and registered only that she was alone. Before dawn, she realised that she was going to be sick. She forced herself to stand up, but didn't have enough strength to walk. She leaned her head over the bare floorboards and tried to vomit. Only a few drops of clear fluid ran from her mouth. Between that night and the next, all she could do was be sick, or try to. Twice she managed to stagger to the bathroom and swallow a few mouthfuls of water, in order to bring it up later. She was still the only one who couldn't vomit ectoplasm. In between, she lay inert on the bed and felt the hard numbness shift inside her. In spite of the cold, she was drenched in sweat.

Some of the others watched her, without trying to help. Sandra came in with Alan, and said something to him that sounded like 'No good to anyone.' The pale creature hung around most of the time. She could feel it draining her, but it pretended to nurse her. It touched her throat with its hollow fingers, and stroked her hair, making gestures of sympathy. Close up, its vacant face was a mosaic, like a cracked window; everything human in it was broken up. Rosalind vomited on its arm, a yellowish bile that scarred it deeply. Or so she thought. There was nobody to share her point of view. Stephen was nowhere in sight. He was probably out looking for someone else. Self-help was all that remained to her.

A day later, she still hadn't eaten anything. But she'd gone on drinking water until eventually she kept it down. Her face in the bathroom mirror was jaundiced. It was probably liver damage, she realised. As soon as she could keep upright, Rosalind struggled from the house and began walking towards the city centre. She could see the post office tower and clock from the roadway. It was getting dark. She watched the clouds moving overhead, a great open stretch of damaged tissue. The smoke of a factory chimney reflected the light from the city. All around her, buildings enclosed the view; but she felt as though she were on a hilltop. The chill of her freedom paralysed her. What cried out in her mind, still, wasn't the atrocity half-realised in her or waiting to be fulfilled in others. It was the simple misery of knowing that the group had created something to unite them. And it had only left each of them feeling more alone.

Sweet nothing

Derek Marlowe

Derek Marlowe was born in London in May 1938. He has written nine novels, the first of which was A Dandy in Aspic *(1966), an espionage novel set partly in East Berlin and featuring a protagonist with the outrageous name of Alexander Eberlin. Some of his work contains elements of horror and fantasy. The very premise of* Memoirs of a Venus Lackey *(1968) is macabre – the narrator speaks to us from his coffin – and* Nightshade *(1975) is set in the twilit world of Haitian voodoo. His elegant prose style contrasts with the corruption and despair that often surface in the subject matter, and he is particularly good at first lines: 'It was going to be the happiest of times'* (Nightshade); *'Within a single hour her absence was opaque'* (Echoes of Celandine, *filmed as* The Disappearance). *Currently he is writing a new novel, and scripting a film based on a novel by Ed McBain.*

One of the finest writers in the English language alive today, Derek Marlowe has published only one other short story, which appeared in Vogue. *In* Sweet Nothing *he evokes atmosphere and emotion as effectively as in* Nightshade. *The execution is subtle but powerful.*

Sweet nothing

Despite the night heat, most of the passengers preferred the conditioned air of their cabins to the warm breeze of the Adriatic. It had been a long voyage and the early romance of being at sea had been replaced by an impatience to reach dry land, and a vow never to set foot on the ship again. The cruise, quite simply, had been a disappointment. The tourists' dreams of dainty intrigues and whispered intimacies had never materialised; an orchestra never played *Perfidia* behind white columns, and the champagne remained unopened as the sun set, ignored.

By the fourth night, less than a dozen passengers strolled the main deck, as if out of duty, silent and bored, before returning below to their whiskies and their paperbacks. By the fifth night, as the ship passed yet another Greek island, only two men could be found, leaning on a rail, staring out at the darkness. Moffat was one of them.

He had been on deck for over an hour, watching the horizon until the island appeared, and then, as lights were seen and houses emerged out of the mist beneath the silhouettes of cypresses, he leaned forward as if wishing to reach out across the dark water. His whole body seemed to strain against the rail, so that the second man, a stranger, observing him, feared that Moffat might suddenly hurl himself into the sea. He moved towards him quickly, then suddenly stopped as he saw Moffat's expression, and realised that whatever it was in the man's eyes, it was not the thought of suicide. It was far more tragic than that.

The stranger looked away, glanced at the island, now a mile away to the stern of the ship, then said quietly:

'Tell me – was she the one we all seek?'

There was no answer. Moffat was attempting to light a cigarette, his hands cupped around the flame. In profile, he looked younger than his 40 years, although his hair was thinning and the tiredness around his eyes would never leave him. His clothes (dark suit, darker coat) revealed no trace of vanity. They had been bought to last.

'Yes,' Moffat said finally. 'Exactly that.'

'And you met her when you were young, on holiday perhaps? You came to that island alone, by chance, and you were bored. You were tired of museums filled with ancient trivia, exhausted by walks in olive groves, the heat was insufferable and you had made up your mind to leave?'

'Yes. That too. Except for the museums. If there were any, I would have avoided them.'

'Naturally.'

'But I couldn't leave immediately. The ship only arrived twice a week. A steamer from the mainland. Smaller than this.'

'And while you waited, you met her?'

'Met her? No. I didn't meet her. I found her. I had rented a bicycle. A green upright Raleigh. The kind midwives ride.'

'And village policemen – '

'Village policemen. Yes. A bicycle like that.'

'Perfect for the island.'

Perfect for the island. It was the very phrase Christoph had used when he free-wheeled it across the quay towards Moffat's table. A bicycle to take him back to his house in the hills two miles away, when night came and the bars in the square closed their shutters. It would put an end to the long nervous walks amid dark, arthritic trees, past the uneven snufflings and sighs, the eyes in the shadows. And so, Moffat had borrowed it for a handful of drachma, intending to keep the Raleigh for no more than two days until the steamer arrived. Instead, it became his possession for more than a month, because, by then, he had found Antonella.

'And how did you find her?'

Antonella. Standing in an iron bath before the southern wall of the house, her hands raising the starched white dress as she turned her eyes towards him, her face moving from shade into light. Her head framed against a flaked green shutter for a brief moment before it was gone, her smile eliminated by folds of white cotton.

'You said you *found* her?'

Antonella. Sitting sideways in front of him, his elbows touching her knees, the shimmer of sunlit hair on her legs, as the bicycle bounced on loose stones and carried them towards the hidden arc of the beach.

'It's the only way I can describe it,' Moffat replied, glancing at the other man, who was now leaning with his back against the rail, arms folded.

'You mean – she was lost?'

'In a way, though I knew where she was. It wasn't that kind of lost.'

'Lost emotionally? Yes. I understand.'

'No, you don't. You don't understand at all. Look, I don't really want to talk about it. I don't know why I began in the first place.'

'It was my fault. I apologise.'

'I don't even know who you are – '

'Don't take offence. I was just making conversation.'

'It's far too private.'

'Of course it is, and I'll say goodnight.'

'Far too private to shout it out to a total stranger.'

'I couldn't agree more. Goodnight.'

'But oh, sweet heaven, I loved her. You *must* believe that.'

The stranger didn't move, except to turn his head slightly towards Moffat and say, almost in a whisper:

'I never doubted it for a moment.'

It was the day when the steamer was due. It usually arrived in the harbour an hour after dawn, but if one was awake, it could be seen long before that, appearing out of the sunrise. Moffat usually watched it from the metal balcony outside his bedroom, but on this particular day, he had clothes to pack and books to retrieve from the garden. He had been reading *Parade's End*, together with a side-salad of Ed McBain, since he could never master the art of completing one book without the distraction of another.

Returning to the house with the books and an abandoned litre of retsina, he discovered that the bicycle had gone. He had left it leaning against a wall dividing the garden and a small orchard belonging to a neighbour. However, realising that he had been somewhat drunk the previous night, Moffat began to walk around the outskirts of the house and then along the path that led to the road. The bicycle was not to be seen, nor was there anyone he could ask. The house was isolated on the slope of a hill, and his neighbour, a retired English clerk, would not arrive until September.

Fortunately, the steamer waited for two hours before sailing and, even on foot, the journey to the harbour took no more than half an hour. And yet the bicycle had to be found and returned to its owner; it was unthinkable that Moffat should leave the island in such disgrace.

Assuming that the thief would take the machine to the road, Moffat had a choice of two directions. South to the harbour or north-east to a small village a mile away. Common sense dictated that he go to the village first, since, if that proved to be futile, he could hurry back to the harbour, seek out the bicycle or Christoph or, happily, both, and still be in time to board the steamer. Carrying his suitcase and his blazer, Moffat set forth on a short cut through a series of olive groves inhabited by goats. Within 15 minutes, he was sweating, having underestimated the heat and the steep paths. He was also lost.

Resting on a wall, he lit a cigarette and looked around. He was in an orchard of apple trees, their grotesque, twisted trunks deep in long grass. There was no sound except for the tinkering of a goat-bell somewhere over there, and an unfamiliar rustling sound, very near to him, a rustling and then silence and then the rustling again. Curious, Moffat stood up and looked around the orchard until his eyes rested on a tree, 30 yards away. The branches were moving.

Moffat stood very still, then slowly lowered his gaze down the tree from leaf to leaf, branch to branch, and then to a pair of sun-tanned legs that seemed to be hanging from within the skirt of the tree, until he saw that the feet were resting on the saddle of a green Raleigh bicycle.

Hurrying to the tree, he shouted: 'Hey! That's *my* bicycle you're standing on!'

Looking up, he saw the face of a girl, her eyes shaded by dark hair. With only the briefest glance at him, she pointed to the top of the tree and said, matter-of-factly: 'Cat.'

Moffat never took the steamer. From that moment, he had no desire to be anywhere except here, in this square-yard in an apple orchard, within the perimeter of the girl's existence.

'It was as immediate as that?' the stranger asked.

'Yes.'

'When one is young – '

'I was 24.'

'And she was?'

'The gentlest, the most beautiful – '

'No. I meant her age?'

'Nineteen.'

'Nineteen . . .'

'It seems such a long time ago. But there hasn't been

a day that I haven't thought about those few short weeks
we spent together. And then the holiday was over and I
went home. I teach school and term had begun.'

Moffat stared across the water as the island disappeared
into darkness, then buttoned up his coat as if to leave.

'Is that all?' the stranger asked in surprise.

'How do you mean?'

'Well, you can't stop now. You've only just begun. What
about walking hand in hand along the tide-edge of empty
beaches at dawn? Or lingering over a glass of wine as the
evening shadows crept through the trees? And what about
waking up to discover her sleeping beside you, the first
wondrous realisation of that? The touchings, the *frissons*.
The sidelong glances, the sweet nothings? Good God, and
that's only half of it! All you offer is a lost bicycle. A girl
up a tree. And a cat – '

'The cat was retrieved unharmed. Don't worry about
it – '

'I'm *not* damn well worried about it. I want to know
more about *you*. And the girl.'

'Oh . . .' Moffat said, somewhat taken aback. 'I see.'

Then he remained silent, self-consciously looking at the
sea below. Next to him, the stranger sighed:

'Look – let's forget about it. I'm not a voyeur. Frankly,
I'd rather have a brandy.'

'But what more is there to say?' Moffat blurted out. 'We
were in love. We were lovers. It was the happiest time in
my whole life and it will never ever happen again. What
else *is* there?'

'She had a name, didn't she?'

'Of course.'

'Well, then . . .?'

'Antonella. Her name was Antonella. She was Italian
from Siena. She was five foot seven. Thin but not too thin.
Blue eyes . . . And she had two brothers. Her father was
dead. Her mother – '

'I don't mean *that*!'

Turning, almost painfully, towards him, Moffat looked

at the stranger and said quietly: 'I know you don't. But how can I describe how she looked when she whispered my name? Her laughter, her enthusiasms? Her sighs? Once I used to be able to – but not any more. I can only remember these things in private. In my mind. You see – I have to.'

'Why is that?'

'Because I have a wife. Obviously she wouldn't understand. How could she? How could she accept a man who hasn't loved as he loved 16 years ago? Who has shared such sweet favours, who was granted such an irreplaceable gift of being loved by – oh, can't you see how inhuman it would be to tell her?'

'Then surely, you can't be happy?'

'If I'd never met Antonella, I would have no regrets. I have two rather plain children of limited intelligence whom I love a little more each day. I have a modest house in the suburbs, a job that pays enough to afford holidays like this. You must realise that I am not an ambitious man. In middle age, I am rather dull. I don't think there is anything in my character that would prompt someone to say: "Ah, yes, I admire Moffat of such and such" or "I do wish I had Moffat's qualities . . ." No. I recognise what I have become. There's no point in hoping it will change.'

'You mustn't say that.'

'But why not? I loved and I was loved. No one can take that away. Whatever happens, no matter how wretched my life is, I have that. You should envy me.'

The stranger stared at him, then suddenly shivered and said: 'I'm going to turn in now. Tomorrow we arrive at Rhodes.'

Moffat didn't speak. He heard the other man murmur goodnight and walk across the deck. A door was opened and then closed.

Alone, Moffat looked down at the white foam spreading out from the ship, the deep troughs of dark water. He was thinking, as always, of Antonella. She was standing on the quay, her hair pushed under a straw hat, leaving only a few strands that drifted across her cheek, touched her neck. She was wearing a blue embroidered dress the colour of her eyes, and in her right hand was a sketch of herself that Moffat had drawn on a day when it had rained and lizards had entered the house. Moffat kissed her and repeated that he would write to her and that, of course, they would see each other again. They were leaving each other and it was madness.

'I love you,' Moffat said and walked away on to the gangplank of the steamer.

Reaching the lower deck, he turned back to the quay to see that Antonella had gone. She was nowhere to be seen.

'I *will* see you again,' Moffat said aloud. 'I promise you that.'

I promise you that. Remembering these words over the years always reduced Moffat to tears. It couldn't be helped. It was not in sadness, however, that he wept. It was far worse than that. The words should never have been said at all.

Unable to bear the emotion, Moffat turned from the rail, walked across the deck and returned below. It was now almost dawn.

Entering his cabin quietly, for fear of waking his wife and children, Moffat poured himself a drink of whisky, from a bottle he always kept within reach, and sat in a chair in the half-light. Too depressed to sleep, he would simply, as was his custom, finish the bottle until he was drunk. He could hear his wife snoring as she lay in her bunk opposite, her hair in pins. The early light from outside highlighted the fullness of her face, the rolls of fat on her neck, the crumb-cakes of mascara clinging to her eyes. Staring at her with cold detachment, Moffat realised how much he hated the woman he had married. Each year she had become more vulgar and more gross; an idle, humourless creature whom he could no longer even bear to touch.

'What are you doing? Where have you been?'

Sweet nothing

Startled, Moffat saw that his wife was awake and was staring at him.

'What have you been doing all night?'

Moffat ignored her and gulped at his drink. There had been moments in the past when he had wanted her dead. Dear God, he thought, oh dear God, I should never have kept that promise. It was the saddest thing I ever did.

'What are you thinking about?' his wife demanded.

On a table, at his elbow, was a photograph of their two children, taken when they were visiting their grandparents in Siena.

'What are you thinking about?' she repeated.

The boy, who had inherited the English features of his father, was called Francis. Named after Moffat's uncle.

'Nothing,' he replied. 'Go back to sleep.'

His daughter, however, easily betrayed her Italian blood by her appearance. The black hair, the dark eyes, the plump arms. She had been christened Antonella.

Named, of course, after Moffat's wife.

The dark land

Michael Marshall Smith

Michael Marshall Smith was born in 1965 in Knutsford, Cheshire. He spent his childhood in the US, Africa and Australia before returning to England in 1975. He studied philosophy and sociology at Cambridge and became involved in the Footlights. Working with the same group – The Throbbs – four years later, he co-wrote and performed two series of the comedy show And Now in Colour . . . *for BBC Radio 4.*

Michael Smith began writing fiction in 1987. He writes quickly. The Dark Land *was written in an afternoon and an evening, which casts some doubt on the late Roald Dahl's theory that you can't write a good short story in less than six months. Michael Smith describes it as the only thing he's ever written based on a dream. He dreamt the first couple of pages and worked the rest of the story out from there. He says now that he has stopped having dreams, or at least remembering them. But far from being short of ideas, he's constantly working on new stories and screenplays and novel-length projects. He defines his fiction as fantasy rather than horror, because he is not setting out to frighten the reader, and does not look to the written word to frighten himself. He reads Stephen King because he enjoys the prose style, and Ramsey Campbell for the 'intense, bizarre dislocation' in his fiction. When he's frightened it's by horror films and real life.*

Michael Smith lives in London where he works as a graphic designer. His ambition is to do something for a living that doesn't make him unhappy. He is very fond of cats, and wishes there were more of them (see The Man Who Drew Cats *in* Dark Voices 2, *reprinted in* Best New Horror 2). Cats *was his first story to appear and another story is now forthcoming in* Fantasy Tales *but* The Dark Land *was his first story to be accepted for publication. It is genuinely frightening.*

The dark land

For want of anything better to do, and in the spirit that keeps my room austerely tidy when there are other things I should be doing, I decided to move my bed. After returning from college I'd redecorated my room, as it had been the same since I'd been about ten, and I'd moved just about everything round except for the bed. I knew it was largely an excuse for not doing anything more constructive but pulled it away from the wall and tried it in another couple of positions.

It was hard work, as one of the legs is rather fragile and the thing had to be virtually lifted off the floor, and after half an hour I was hot and irritated and becoming more and more convinced that its original position had been the optimal, and indeed the only, place to put it. And it was as I struggled to shove it back up against the wall that I began to feel a bit strange. When it was finally back in place I sat down on it, feeling light-headed and a bit ill and I suppose basically I just drifted off to sleep.

I don't know if the bed is part of it in some way. I only mention it because it seems important, and because I guess that it was while I was asleep on it that it all began. After a while I woke up, half-remembering a dream in which I had been doing nothing more than lying on my bed remembering that my parents had said that they were going to extend the wood panelling on the downstairs hall walls. For a few moments I was disorientated, confused by being in the same place in reality as I had been in the dream, and then I drifted off again.

Some time later I awoke again, feeling very sluggish and slightly nauseous. I found it very difficult to haul my mind up from sleep, but eventually stood up and lurched across the room to the sink to get a glass of water, rubbing my eyes and feeling very rough. Maybe I was going down with something. I decided that a cup of tea would be a good idea, and headed out of the bedroom to go downstairs to the kitchen to make one.

As I reached the top of the stairs I remembered the dream about the panelling and wondered vaguely where a strange idea like that could have come from. I'd worked hard for my psychology paper at college, and was fairly confident that Freud hadn't felt that wood panelling was even worth a mention. I trudged downstairs, still feeling a bit strange, my thoughts dislocated and confused.

Then I stopped, open-mouthed, and stared around me. They really *had* extended the panelling. It used to only go about eight feet up the wall, but it now soared right up to the front hall ceiling, which is two floors high. And they'd done it in exactly the same wood as the original panelling: there wasn't a join to be seen. How the hell had they managed that? Come to that, *when* the hell had they managed that? It hadn't been there that morning, both my parents were at work and would be for hours and . . . well, it was just impossible, wasn't it? I reached out and touched the wood, marvelling at how even the grain was the same, and that the new wood looked just as aged as the original, which had been there fifty years.

As I struggled to get my still sluggish mind in gear surprise suddenly gave way to astonishment. Wait a minute, I thought, that isn't right. There hadn't used to be *any* panelling in the hall. It used just to be white walls. Sure, the stairs were panelled in wood, but the walls were just plain white plaster. How the hell could I have forgotten that? What had made me think that the front hall had been panelled, and think it so unquestioningly? I could now remember that I'd recently noticed, sensitised to these things as I was by having recently repainted my room, that the white paint in the hall was rather dirty, especially round the light switches. So what was all this panelling doing here? Where had it come from, and when, for Christ's sake? And why had I been so sure that at least some of it had always been there?

I walked slowly into the kitchen, casting bewildered backward glances at the walls. I heard a soft clinking sound outside and walked to the back door, too puzzled about the front hall to even notice that it was rather late for a milk delivery. The back door, which like the front door opens out onto the driveway, is in a little corridor full of gardening implements, shoes and tools which leads off the kitchen to the garage. I threaded my way through these and wrenched the stiff door open.

As soon as it was open I reeled backwards from the light and unthinkingly crouched just inside the back hall. Then I realised that it wasn't even that bright outside: it was late afternoon and the light was muted, but everything seemed very intense, like colours before a storm. Odd, but not odd enough to throw yourself to the ground over, I thought as I stood up. But it had been the milkman after all, for there was our milk bottle holder with four bottles of milk in it. Only they weren't milk bottles, but large American-style quart containers somehow jammed into slots meant to take pints. And someone had taken the silver tops off.

Something at the edge of my vision caught my attention and I looked up towards the top of the driveway. There, about thirty yards away, were two children, one fat and on a bike, the other slim and standing. I was seized with a sudden irrational fury and started quickly up the drive towards them, convinced that the clinking sound I'd heard was them stealing the tops off the milk.

I had covered scarcely five yards when from behind me someone who'd been at my school walked quickly and inexplicably past me up the drive, staring straight ahead. I couldn't remember his name, had barely known him, in fact. He'd been two or three years older than me, and I'd completely forgotten that he'd existed, but as I stared after him I remembered that he'd been one of the more amiable seniors. I could recall being proud of having some small kind of communication with one of the big boys and how it had made me feel a bit older myself, more a man of the world, less of a kid. And I remembered the way he used to greet my yelling a nickname greeting at him, a half-smile and the raising of an eyebrow.

All this came back with the instantaneous impact of memory, but something wasn't right. He didn't smile at all, or even seem to register that I was there. I felt oddly disturbed and chilled, not by the genuinely strange fact that he was there at all, or that he was wearing school athletic gear when he must have left the school seven years ago, but because he didn't smile and tilt his head back the way he used to. It was so bizarre that I wondered briefly if I was dreaming, but if you can ask yourself the question you always know the answer, and I wasn't.

My attention was distracted on the other side by a reflection in the glass of the window in the back hallway. A man with glasses, a chubby face and blond hair that looked as if it had been cut with a basin seemed to be standing behind me, carrying a bicycle. I whirled round to face where he should have been, but he wasn't there. Then I remembered the kids at the top of the driveway and, seeing that they were still standing motionless, began to shout at them again, needing something to take my bewilderment out on.

Almost immediately a tall slim man in a dark suit came walking down the drive. I don't know if it was a trick of the light in the gathering dusk, but I couldn't seem to fix on his face. In retrospect it was as if an unnatural shadow hung there but at the time my eyes just seemed to slide off it as if it were slippery, or made of ice.

'Stop shouting at them,' the man said as he passed me, walking towards the back door. I stared at him open-mouthed. 'They're not doing anything wrong. Leave them alone.'

The kids took themselves off, the one walking beside the other on the bike, and I turned to the suited man, anxious, for some reason, to placate him, and yet at the same time slightly outraged at his invasion of our property.

'I'm sorry,' I said. 'It's just, well, I'm a bit thrown. I thought I saw someone I knew in the drive. Did you see him? Sort of wavy brown hair, athletics gear?'

For some reason I thought that the man would say that he had, and that that would make me feel better, but all I got was a curt 'No'. I was by now looking at his back as he entered the back hallway.

'Shall we go into your old house then?' asked another voice, clearly talking to the suited man, and I saw that someone else was in the back hall: the man with the blond hair and glasses. And he really was carrying a bicycle, for God's sake.

'What?' I said incredulously, and hurried after them, catching a glimpse of the suited man's face. 'But it's you . . .' I continued, baffled, as I realised that the man in the suit was the man who had been in athletics gear. The two men walked straight into the kitchen and I followed them, quietly, and seemingly impotently, enraged. *Was* this his old house? Even if it was, wasn't it customary to ask the current occupants if you fancied a visit?

The suited man was by now peering round the kitchen, where for some reason everything looked very messy. He

poked at some fried rice I'd left in a frying pan on the
stove, or at least I seemed to have left it there, though
I wasn't sure when I would have done so. Again I felt
the urge to placate and hoped he would eat some, but
he just grimaced with distaste and joined the other man
at the window looking out onto the drive, hands on hips,
his back to me.

'Dear God,' he muttered, and the other man grunted in
agreement.

I noticed that I'd picked up the milk from outside the
back door, and appeared to have spilt some of it on the
floor. I tried to clean it up with a piece of kitchen roll
which seemed very dirty and yellowed as if with age, my
mind aching under the strain of trying to work out what
the hell was going on. I felt that there must be some
sense to it somewhere, some logic of the situation that
I was missing. Even if he had lived here once he had
no right to just march in here with his friend like that,
but I realised as I continued ineffectively trying to swab
up the milk before he noticed it (why?) that there was
something far wronger than a mere breach of protocol
going on here. The suited man looked about thirty-five,
far older then he should have been if he was indeed the
man I'd been to school with, and yet far too young to
ever have lived here, as between our family and the
people we'd bought it from, the house's last 40 years
were accounted for. So how the hell could it be his
house? There was no way. And was it him anyway?
Apart from being too old, it looked like him, but was it
actually *him*?

As I straightened up, having done the best I could with
the milk, I staggered slightly, feeling very disorientated
and strange, my perception both heightened and jumbled
at the same time, as if I was very drunk. Everything
seemed to have a nightmarish intensity and exaggerated
emotional charge, and yet there also seemed to be gaps
in what I was perceiving, as if I was only taking in an
edited version of what was going on. Things began to

appear to jump from one state to another, with the bits
in between, the becoming, missed out like a series of
jump cuts. I felt hot and dizzy and the kitchen looked
small and indescribably messy and the orange paint of
the walls seemed to jump in at me beneath a low swaying
ceiling. I wondered confusedly if I was seeing the kitchen
as they saw it, and then immediately wondered what I
meant by that.

All the time they just stood there, turning round occasionally to stare balefully at me, radiating distaste and
impatience. Obviously they were waiting for something.
But what? What was going on? Noticing I still had the
piece of kitchen roll in my hand I stepped over all the
rubbish on the floor – what the hell had been going on
in this kitchen? – to put it in the overflowing bin. Then,
squeezing my temples with my fingers and struggling both
to concentrate and to stand upright against the weight of
the air I turned towards the men.

'L-look', I stuttered, 'what the hell is going on?' and
immediately wished I hadn't. There was a pause and then
the suited man turned his head very slowly towards me and
it kept turning and turning until he was facing me while his
body stayed facing the other way. I could feel my stomach
trying to crawl away and fought against the gagging. He'd
done that deliberately, done it because he knew it would
make me want to throw up, and I thought he might just
be right.

'Why don't you just shut up?' he snarled, the words
squirming from his mouth like rats out of the stomach
of something recently dead, and twisted his head slowly
back round through 180 degrees until he was looking out
onto the drive once more.

Meanwhile, the mess in the kitchen seemed to be getting
worse. Every time I looked there were more dirty pans and
bits of rubbish and old food on the floor. My head was
getting thicker and heavier and felt like it was slipping
away from me. I half fell against the fridge and clung
to it, almost pulling it off the wall, and began to cry,

my tears cutting channels in the thick grime on the fridge door. I dimly remembered that we'd bought a new fridge the week before but they must have changed it because this one looked like something out of the fifties, but it was hard to tell because it was swimming back and forth and there was a lot of white in my eyes and I couldn't see past it. They were both watching me now.

Suddenly a terrible jangling pierced my ear, as if someone were hammering a pencil into it. It happened again and I recognised it first as a sound and not a blow after all, and then as the doorbell. Someone was at the front door.

The two men glanced at each other and then the blond one nodded. The suited man turned to me.

'Do you know what that is?' he asked.

'Yes, it's the front door,' I said, trying to please him.

'Yes. So you'd better answer it, hadn't you? Answer the *door*.'

'Should I answer it?' I said, stupidly. I just couldn't seem to remember what words meant any more.

'*Yes*,' he grated and then picked up a mug, my mug, the mug I came down, I remembered randomly, to put tea in, and hurled it at me. It smashed into the fridge door by my face. I struggled to stand upright, my head aching and ears ringing, hearing a soft crump as a fragment of the mug broke under my foot. Then the doorbell jangled again, its harsh sharpness making me realise how muted sounds had been becoming. I fell rather than stepped towards the kitchen door, sliding across the front of the fridge, my feet tangling in the boxes and cartons that now seemed to cover the filthy floor. I could feel the orange of the walls seeping in through my ears and mouth and kept missing whole seconds as if I was blacking out and coming to like a stroboscope. As I banged into the door and grabbed the handle to hold myself up I heard the blond man say, 'He may not go through. If he does, we wait.'

But it didn't mean anything to me. None of it did.

Stepping clumsily over more piles of rubbish I headed for the front door. The chime of the doorbell had pushed the air hard and I could see it coming towards me in waves. Ducking, I slipped on the mat and almost fell into the living room on hands and knees. But it was getting dark in there, I could see, really dark, and I could hear the plants talking. I couldn't catch the words, but they were there, beneath the night sounds and a soft rustling which sounded a hundred yards away. The living room must have grown, I thought groggily, picking myself up and turning myself to the front door as the bell clanged again. It should be about four paces across the hall from the living room door to the front door but I thought it was only going to take one and then it took twenty, past all the panelling and over the huge folds in the mat. And then I had my hand on the doorknob and then the door was open and I stepped out of the house.

'Oh, hello, Michael. I thought someone must be in, because all the lights were on.'

'Wuh?' I said, blinking in the remnants of sunlight, breathless with the feeling of my mind soaring up towards normality like a runaway lift. Then, 'Sorry?'

'I hope I didn't disturb you?' the woman standing in front of me said, and I now recognised her to be Mrs Steinburg, the woman who brings us our catfood in bulk.

'No, no, that's fine. Fine,' I said, looking covertly behind me into the hall, which was solid and unpanelled and four paces wide and led to the living room which was light and about ten yards deep. Good. Think about that later. Deal with the cat woman.

'I've brought your delivery,' she said. 'Look, are you all right?'

'Yes. I'm fine,' I replied, smiling broadly. 'I . . . er . . .' I . . . er . . . what? 'I . . . er . . . just nodded off for a moment, in the kitchen. I still feel a bit, you know . . .'

'Of course.' Mrs Steinburg smiled. I followed her up the drive and heaved the box of catfood out of the back of her van, looking carefully back at the house. There was nothing to see. I thanked her and then carried the box back down the drive as she drove off.

I walked back into the house and shut the front door behind me. I felt absolutely fine. I walked into the kitchen. Normal. It didn't even occur to me to wonder if the two men would still be there. They weren't. I must just have fallen asleep making tea, and then struggled over to the front door to open it while still half asleep. I could remember asking myself if it was a dream and thinking it wasn't but that just showed how wrong you could be, didn't it? It had been unusually vivid, and it was odd how I'd been suddenly awake and all right again as soon as I stepped out of the front door. Odd, and a bit disconcerting. But here I was in the kitchen again and everything was normal, clean and tidy, spick and span, with all the rubbish in the bin and the pans in the right places and the milk in the fridge and a smashed mug on the floor.

Suddenly I didn't feel quite so good. It was my mug, and it was smashed, on the floor, at the bottom of the fridge. Now how had that happened? Maybe I'd fallen asleep holding it (fallen asleep standing up with a mug in my hand? Now how likely was that?), maybe I'd knocked it over waking up and incorporated the sound into my dream (better, better, but where exactly was I supposed to have fallen asleep? Just leaning against the counter, or actually stretched out on it with the kettle as a pillow?). Then I noticed the fridge door.

There was a little dent in it, with a couple of flecks of paint missing. At about head height.

That wasn't good. That wasn't good at all. In fact it felt as if someone had just punched a hole in my chest and poured icy water into it. But everything else was all right, wasn't it? I cleared up the mug and switched the kettle on and while it was boiling wandered into the hall and the living room. Everything was fine, tidy, normal. Super. Back into the kitchen. The same. Great. Apart from a little dent in the fridge door at about head height.

I made my cup of tea, though not in my mug of course, and drank it standing looking out of the kitchen window at the drive, feeling unsettled and nervous, and unsure of what to do with either of those emotions. Even if it had been a dream, it was odd, particularly the way it had fought so hard against melting away. Maybe I was much more tired than I realised. Or maybe I was ill. But I felt fine, physically at least.

I carried the box of catfood into the pantry, unpacked it, and stacked the cans in the corner. Then I switched the kettle on for another cup of tea. Suddenly my heart seemed to stop and before I had time to realise why, the cause repeated itself. A soft chinking noise outside the back door.

I moved quickly to the window and looked out. Nothing. I craned my neck, trying to see round to the back door, but could only see the large pile of firewood that lay to one side of it. The noise again.

Clenching my fists I walked slowly into the back hallway and listened. Silence, except for the sound of blood beating in my ears. My stomach knotting and hands moist with perspiration. Then I grabbed the knob and swung the door open. Stillness. Just a rectangle of late afternoon light, a patch of driveway, a dark hedge waving quietly. I stepped out into the drive.

A very faint crunching noise. And then again. Sounded almost like pebbles rubbing against each other. Again. I looked more closely at the drive, peering at the actual stones, and then noticed that a very small patch about ten yards in front of me appeared to be moving slightly, wriggling, almost. As I watched they stopped, and then the sound came again and another patch, about a yard closer than the first, stirred briefly. As if registering the weight of invisible feet. I was so engrossed that I didn't notice the whistling straight away. When I did, I looked up.

The blond man was back. Standing at the top of the driveway, carrying a bicycle with the wheels slowly spinning in the dusk, whistling the top line of two in perfect harmony, the lower line just the wind. As I stared at him, backing slowly towards the house, the crunching noise got louder and louder and then the suited man was standing with his nose almost touching mine.

'Hello again,' he said.

The blond man started down the driveway, smiling.

'Hello again indeed,' he said. 'Come on, in we go.'

Suddenly I realised that the very last thing in the world I should do was let those two back into the house. I leapt through the back door back into the hallway. The suited man, caught by surprise, started forward but I was quick and whipped the door shut in his face and locked it. That felt very good but then he started banging on the door very hard, ridiculously hard, grotesquely hard, and I noticed that to my right the kitchen was getting messy again and the fridge was old and I could barely see out of the window because it was so grimy and a slight flicker made me think that maybe I'd missed the smallest fraction of a second and I realised that it really hadn't been a fucking dream and I was back there, and I was back there because I'd come in through the back door again. As I backed into the kitchen I tripped and fell, sprawling amongst the cartons and bacon rind and the dirt and was that puke, for Christ's sake? The banging on the back door got louder and louder and louder. He was going to break it. He was going to break the fucking door down. I'd let them back and they had to come in through the back door. I'd come in through the wrong door . . .

Suddenly realising what I must do, I scrambled up and kicked my way through the rubbish towards the door to the front hall. The fridge door swung open in my way and the inside was dark and dirty and there was something rotted in there but I slammed it out of the way, biting hard on my lip to keep my head clear. I had to get to the front door, I had to open it, step out, and then step back in again. That was the right door. And I had to do it soon, before the back door broke and let them in. As I ran out of the kitchen into the front hall I could already hear a splintering quality to the sound of the blows. And the back door was about two inches thick.

The hallway was worse than I expected. I came to a halt, at first unable to even see the front door. Then I thought that I must be looking in the wrong direction but I wasn't, because there it was over to the left where it was supposed to be, but the angles were all wrong and to see it I had to look behind me and to the right, although when I saw it I could see that it was still over there to the left. And it looked so close, could it really be less than a yard away, but when I held my hand out to it I groped into nothing, my hand still in front of the door when it should have been past it. I stared wildly around me, disorientated and unsure somehow even of which way to go. Then the banging behind me got even louder, probably as the blond man joined in, and this helped marginally to restore my sense of direction. I found the door again, concentrated hard on its apparent position and started to walk towards it. I immediately fell over, because the floor was much lower than I expected, and in fact must be tilted in some way as one of my legs reached it easily enough, although it looked flat and level. I pulled myself up onto my knees and found I was looking at a sort of sloped wall between the wall and the ceiling, a wall which bent back from the wall and yet out from the ceiling. And the door was still over there on the left, although to see it I now had to look straight ahead and up.

Then I noticed another sound beneath the eternal banging and whirled round to face the direction it was coming from. I found that I was looking through the living room door and that it gave into sheer darkness, a darkness which was seeping out into the hallway like smoke, clinging to the angles in the air like the inside of a dark prism. I heard the noise again and it was a deep rumbling growling far far away in there, almost obscured by the night noises and the sound of vegetation moving in the wind. It didn't seem to be getting any closer but I knew that was because the living room now extended out far beyond, into hundreds and hundreds of miles of dense forest jungle, and as I listened carefully I could hear the gurgling of some dark river far off to the right, mixing with the warm rustling of the breeze in the darkness. It sounded very peaceful and for a moment I was still, transfixed.

Then the sound of a violently splintering crack wrenched me away and I turned my back on the living room and flailed towards where the front door must be. The hall table loomed above me and I thought I could walk upright beneath it but tripped over it trying and fell again, headlong onto the cool floorboards. The mat had moved, no, was moving, sliding slowly up the stairs like a draught and as I rolled over and looked at the ceiling I saw the floor coming towards me, the walls shortening in little jerks. Another splintering thud and now I had no idea which way was up.

As I lay there panting a clear cool waft of air stroked my cheek. At first I thought that it must have come from the living room, although it had been warm in there, but then I remembered rather than saw that I was lying on the floor and that the breeze must be a draught coming under the front door. I must nearly be there. I looked all around me but all I could see was panelling and floor and what was behind me. I closed my eyes and tried to grope for it but it was even worse inside so I opened them again. Then I caught a glimpse of the door, far away, obscured from view round a corner but visible once you knew where to look. On impulse I reached my hand out in not quite the opposite direction and felt it fall upon warm grainy wood. The door, the bloody door. I'd found the front door.

I pulled myself along the floor towards it and tried to stand up. I got no more than a few inches before I fell back down again. I tried again with the same result, feeling as if I was trying to do something very unnatural and bizarre. Again, and this time I reached a semi-crouching position, muscles straining. I started to slump down again but as I did so I threw myself forwards and found myself curled up, my feet a couple of feet from the floor, lying on the door. Forcing my mind not to even try to come to terms with this I groped by my side and found the doorknob. I tried to twist it but the sweat on my hands made them spin uselessly on the shiny metal. I wiped them on my shirt and tried again and this time I got some purchase and heard the catch withdraw as the knob turned. Exultantly I tugged at it as with a tremendous crash the back door finally gave way.

The door wouldn't budge. Panicking, I tried again. Nothing. By peering down the crack I could see that no lock or bolt was impeding it, so why wouldn't it bloody move?

Footsteps in the back hall. Suddenly I realised that I was lying on the door, and trying to pull it towards me against my own weight. Silly me. The footsteps reached the kitchen.

I rolled over off the door onto the wall beside it and reached for the handle but I'd gone too far. As the footsteps came closer, towards the kitchen door into the hall, I scrambled across the slippery wall, grabbed and twisted the doorknob with all my strength. It opened just as they entered the hall and I rolled out through it, fell and landed awkwardly and painfully on something hard and bristly and for a few moments had no clear idea of where or who I was and just lay there fighting for breath.

After some time I sat up slowly. I was sitting on the doormat, my back to the front door. At the top of the drive a passing couple were staring at me curiously. I stood up and smiled, trying to suggest that I often sat there and that they ought to try it as it really was a lot of fun, hoping to God that they hadn't seen me fall there from about two-thirds of the way up the door. They smiled back and carried on walking, mollified or maybe even hurrying off home to try it for themselves, for all I knew. I turned hesitantly back towards the door and looked in.

It had worked. It was all all right again. The mat was on the floor, right angles looked like 90 degrees again and the ceiling was back where it was supposed to be. I stepped back a pace and looked across at the back door. It had been utterly smashed and now looked like little more than an extension of the firewood pile.

I walked back into the hall through the front door, the right door, and shut it behind me. I wandered carefully and quietly into the living room and the kitchen. Everything was fine, everything was normal. Just a nice normal house. If you came in through the right door.

The wrong door was in about a thousand pieces now, of course. I thought about that for some time, with a cup of tea and what felt like my first cigarette in months. Less than an hour had elapsed, I saw with frank disbelief, since I'd first come downstairs.

The wrong door. It was coming in through there that took me to wherever or whatever it was that the house became. Coming in through the front door brought me back to wherever it was that I normally lived. So presumably I was safe so long as I didn't leave the house and come back in through the back door. They couldn't get me.

Presumably. But I didn't like having that door in pieces. The wrong door, the door through which they had to come, was in pieces. Being safe was only part of the problem. I wasn't going to feel *secure* until that portal was well and truly closed. It wasn't precisely clear, however, what I could do about that.

I walked into the back hall and looked nervously out through the wreckage onto the drive. Everything was fine. There was nothing I needed protecting from. But I didn't like it. Did it have to be me who came through it, or what if maybe a falling leaf or even just a soft breeze came inside? Would that be enough? Could I take the risk?

As I stood there indecisively I noticed once more the pile of firewood propped up against the outside wall of the back hall. I probably still wouldn't have thought of it had not a very large proportion of the pile been old thick planks. I looked at the tool shelf on the inside wall and saw a hammer and a big box of good long nails. Then I looked at the wood again.

I could nail the damn thing shut.

I flicked my cigarette butt out onto the drive and rolled up my sleeves. The hammer was big and heavy, which was just as well because when I nailed the planks across the door frame I'd be hammering into solid brickwork. I was going to have to board right the way up but that was all right as there were loads of planks, and if I reinforced it enough it should be well-nigh impregnable. Feeling much better now that I had a way of sealing off the door, I set to work. I may even have hummed.

Kneeling just inside the door, I reached out and began pulling planks in, taking care to select the thickest and least weathered. I judged that I'd need about thirty-five to make the doorway really secured, although that was largely guesswork as I'd never tried to turn the back hall into a fortress before. Getting the planks in was heavy work as I had to stretch out to reach them, and I began to get hot and tired, and anxious to begin the nailing. Outside it was getting darker as the evening began, and the air was very cool and still.

As the pile in the back hall increased in size it became more difficult still, and I had to lean further and further out to reach the next plank, and this made me nervous. I was still inside, my feet were still on the ground in the back hall. I wasn't 'coming back in', I was just leaning out and then, well, sort of coming back in but not really, because my feet never left the back hall, did they? But it made me nervous, and I began to work quicker and quicker, perspiration running down my face and arms as, clinging to the doorframe with my left hand, I stretched out to bring the last few boards in. I felt tired and irritated and was dying for a smoke but couldn't take the time: I was anxious to start nailing. Thirty-one, thirty-two, just a couple more. Now the last one I could possibly reach: that would have to be enough. Hooking my left foot behind the frame and gripping it hard with my left hand I stretched out towards the plank, my waving fingers little more than an inch from the end. Just a little further forward: I let my hooking foot slide round slightly, let my fingers slip round half an inch and tried to extend my back as far as it would go. My fingers just scraping the end I tried a last yearning lunge.

And then suddenly a stray thought struck me. Here I was, pulled out as if on some invisible rack: why on earth hadn't I just gone out of the front door, picked up piles of wood and brought them back into the house through the front door? It would have been easier, it would have been quicker, and it wouldn't have involved all this monkeying around at the wrong door. Not that it mattered now, because as it happened even if I didn't get this last plank I'd probably have plenty, but I wouldn't have been so hot and tired and it was also a bit worrying that in my haste I'd been putting myself in needless danger. I'd better slow down, calm down, take a rest.

An unimportant, contemplative thought. But one that distracted me for a fraction of a second too long. As

I finally got the tips of my fingers round the plank I realised with horror that my other fingers, the ones on the doorframe, were slipping. I was slowly sliding forwards. Desperately I tried to scrabble with my fingers, but my hands were too sweaty and the doorframe itself was slippery now. I felt the tendons in my hand stretch as I tried to defy my centre of gravity and think my weight backwards, and then suddenly my forehead walloped onto the ground and I was lying flat on my face.

I was up in a second, and I swear to God that both feet never left the hall floor at once. I hurled myself back into the hallway, clutching that last bloody piece of wood without even noticing it.

Panting and almost sobbing with nervous hysteria I crouched in the doorframe, looking out. Everything looked normal. The driveway was quiet, the pebbles were still and there was none of the faint deadening of sound that I associated with the other place. I was furious with myself for having taken the risk, for not having thought to bring them in through the front door, and especially for falling, which had been bloody painful quite apart from anything else. But I hadn't fallen out, not really. I hadn't come back in, as such. The drive was fine, the kitchen was fine. Everything was fine.

Soothed by the sounds of early evening traffic in the distance, my heart gradually slowing down to only about twice its normal rate, I began to feel a bit better and had a quiet cup of tea, perched on the pile of planks. In falling over my right foot had caught the tool shelf and there were nails all over the place, inside and out, but there were plenty left and the ones outside could bloody stay there. I wasn't going to make the same damnfool mistake twice.

Gathering up the hammer and a fistful of nails I laid a plank across the door and started work. Getting the nails through the wood and into the masonry was even harder than I'd expected, but in a couple of minutes it was in place, and felt very solid. I heaved another plank into place and set about securing it. This was actually going to work.

After half an hour I was into the swing of it and the wood now reached almost halfway up the doorframe. My arms aching and head ringing from the hammering, which was very loud in the confined space of the back hall, I had a cigarette leaning on the completed section, staring blankly out onto the drive. I was jolted back from reverie by the realisation that a piece of dust or something must have landed in my eye, slightly distorting my vision, and I blinked to remove it. But it didn't go. It didn't hurt, just made a small patch of the drive up near the road look a bit ruffled. I rubbed and shut both eyes individually and discovered with mounting unease that the distortion was present in both.

I stood upright. Something was definitely going on at the top of the drive. The patch still looked ruffled, as if seen through a heat haze, and whichever way I turned my head it stayed in the same place. It was flickering very slightly now too, like a bad quality film print. But the flecks weren't white, they were dark. I rubbed my eyes hard again, but once I'd stopped seeing stars I saw that the effect was still there, and I stared hard at it, trying to discern something that I could interpret. The flecks seemed to organize into broken and shifting vertical lines as I watched, as if something were hidden behind a curtain of rain, rain so coloured as to make up a picture of that patch of the drive. This impression gradually strengthened until it was like looking at one of those plastic strip 'doors', where you walk through the hanging strips. It was as if there was one of those at the top of the drive with a patch of driveway pictured on it in living three dimensions, with something moving just the other side of it.

Then suddenly the balance shifted, like one of those drawings made up of black and white dots where if you stare at it long enough you can see a Dalmatian. I dropped to my knees behind the partially completed barrier. Fear was no longer a word I had any use for. They were back.

Standing at the top of the drive, their images somehow

both underlying and superimposed on it as if the two were woven together, were the man in the suit and the blond man. They were standing in a frozen and unnatural position, like a freeze-frame in a very old home movie, their faces pallid and washed out, the colouring uneven, the image flickering and dancing in front of my eyes. And still they stood, not there, and yet in some sense there.

As I stared, transfixed, I noticed that the suited man's foot appeared to be moving. It was hard to focus on, and happening bizarrely slowly, but it was moving, gradually leaving the ground. Then, as over the course of several minutes it was raised and then lowered back onto the ground a couple of feet in front of its original position, leaving the man's body leaning slightly forward, I realised what I was seeing. In extraordinary and flickering slow motion, somehow projected onto the drive, the suited man was beginning to walk down towards the house. Except that the image wasn't flickering so much any more, the colours were stronger, and I could no longer see the driveway through them. Somehow they were coming back through. I thought I'd got away with it, but I hadn't. I'd fallen out. Not very far by anyone's standards, but far enough. Far enough to have come back in through the wrong door. And now they were tearing their way back into the world, or hauling me back towards theirs. And very very slowly they were getting closer.

Fighting to stay calm I grabbed a plank, put it into position above the others and nailed it into place. Then another, and another, not pausing for breath or thought. Through the narrowing gap I could see them getting closer and they didn't look anything like two-dimensional photographs any longer and they were moving quicker now too. Then as I leaned towards the kitchen for a plank I saw that there was a single dusty carton on the floor. It had started.

I smacked another plank into place and hammered it down. The suited man and the blond man were now real again, and they were also much closer, though still moving at a weirdly graceful tenth of normal speed. Hammering wildly now, ignoring increasingly frequent whacks on the fingers, I cast occasional monitoring glances aside into the kitchen. The fridge was beginning to look a bit strange, the stark nineties geometry softening, regressing, and the rubbish was gathering. I never saw any of it arrive, but each time I looked there was another piece of cardboard, a few more scraps, one more layer of grime. It had barely started, and was still happening very slowly, maybe because I'd barely fallen out, but it was happening. The house was going over.

And I kept right on hammering. Obviously what I had to do at some point was run to the front door, go out and come back in again, come in through the right door. But that could wait, would have to wait. It was all developing very slowly this time and I still felt completely clear-headed. What I had to do first was seal off the back door, and soon. The two men, always at the vanguard of the change, were well and truly here, and getting closer all the time. I had to make sure that the back door was secure against anything those two could do to it for long enough for me to get to the front door. I had no idea what the front hall would be like by the time I got there and if I left the back door unfinished and got caught up in the front hall trying to get to the door I'd be in real trouble.

So I slammed planks into place as fast as I could. Outside they got steadily closer and inside another carton appeared in the kitchen. As I jammed the last horizontal board into place the suited man and the blond man were only a couple of yards away, now moving at full pace, and I'd barely nailed it in before the first blow crashed into it, bending it and making me leap back with shock. I hurriedly picked up more wood and started to place planks over the barrier in vertical slats and crosses, nailing them in hard, reinforcing and making sure that they were securely fastened to the wall on all sides, furiously hammering and building. After a while I couldn't feel the ache in my back or see the blood on my hands: all I could hear was the beating of the hammer, and all I could see were the heads of the nails as I piled more and more wood onto the barrier. I had wood to spare – I hadn't even needed that last bloody plank – and by the time I finished it was four planks thick in some places, and the reinforcing strips spread several feet either side of the frame. I used the last three pieces as bracing struts, forcing them horizontally across the hallway, one end of each lodged in niches in the barrier, the other jammed tight against the opposite wall.

Finally it was finished and I stood back and looked at it. It looked pretty damn solid.

'Let's see you get through that then, you bastards,' I said quietly, half sitting and half collapsing to the ground.

After a moment I noticed how quiet it was. At some point they must have stopped banging against the door. How long ago I had no idea. I'd been making far too much noise to notice, and my ears were still ringing. I put my ear against the barrier and listened. Silence. I lit a cigarette and let tiredness and a blessed feeling of safeness wash over me. The sound of the match striking was slightly muted, but that could've been the ringing in my ears as much as anything and the kitchen looked pretty grubby but no more than that. And I felt fine.

Vaguely wondering what the two outside were up to, whether there was any chance that they might, not realising that I understood about the right door and the wrong door, have given up and be waiting for the change to take its course, I sat and finished my cigarette, actually savouring the feeling of being balanced between two worlds, secure in the knowledge that in a moment I would just walk out that front door and the house would come back and none of it would matter a damn.

Eventually I stood up. I was really going to ache tomorrow, I thought as I stepped into the kitchen, narrowly avoiding a large black spider that scuttled out of one of the cartons. The floor was getting very messy now, with scraps of dried-up rotted meat covered with the corpses of dead maggots and small piles of stuff I really didn't want to look at too closely. Skirting the rubbish I walked over to the door past the now bizarrely misshapen fridge and into the front hall.

The hallway was still clear, and as far as I could see, utterly normal. As I crossed it towards the front door, anxious now to get the whole thing over with, and wondering how I was going to explain the state of the back door to my family, I noticed a very faint tapping sound in the far distance. After a moment it stopped, and then restarted from a slightly different direction. Odd, but scarcely a primary concern. Right now my priority was getting out of that front door before the hall got any stranger.

Feeling like an actor about to bound onto stage, and looking forward very much to looking out onto the real world, I reached out to the doorknob, twisted it and pulled it towards me, smiling.

At first I couldn't take it in. I couldn't understand why instead of the driveway all I could see was brown. Brown flatness. Then as I adjusted my focal length, pulling it in for something much closer than the drive I'd been expecting, I began to realise, because the view looked rather familiar. I'd seen something like it very recently.

It was a barrier. An impregnable wooden barrier nailed across the door into the walls from the outside. Now I knew what they'd been doing as I finished nailing them out. They'd been nailing me in.

I tried everything I could think of against that barrier, my fists, my shoulder, a chair. It was there to stay. I couldn't get out. I couldn't come back in through the right door and for the moment they couldn't get in through the wrong door. A sort of stalemate. But a very poor sort for me, because they were much the stronger and getting more so all the time, because the house was still going over and now I couldn't stop it.

I walked into the kitchen, rubbing my bruised shoulder and thinking furiously. There had to be something I could do, and I had to do it fast. The change was speeding up.

Although the hall still looked normal the kitchen was now filthy, and the fifties fridge was back. In the background I could still hear the faint tapping noise. Maybe they were trying to get in through the roof.

I had to get out, had to find a way. Come on, lateral thinking. You leave a house by a door. How else? No other way. You always leave by a door. But is there any other way you *could* leave? The doors . . . Christ. The windows. What about the windows? If there was a right door and a wrong door, maybe there were right and wrong windows too, and maybe the right ones looked out onto the real world. Maybe, just maybe, you could smash one and then climb out and then back in again. Maybe that would work.

I had no idea whether it would or not, I wasn't kidding myself that I understood anything, and God alone knew where I might land if I chose the wrong window. Perhaps I'd go out the wrong one and then be chased round the house by the two maniacs outside as I tried to find a right window to break back in through. That would be a barrel of laughs, wouldn't it? That would be just Fun City. But what choice did I have? Through the square window today, children, I thought crazily, and ran into the living room, heading for the big picture window.

I don't know how I could not have made the connection. Maybe because the taps were so quiet. I just stood in the living room, my mouth open. This time they were one jump ahead. They'd boarded up the bloody windows.

I ran into the hall, the dining room, upstairs to the bedrooms. Every single window was boarded up. I knew where they'd got the nails from, I'd spilt more than enough when I fell, but how . . . Then I realised how they'd nailed them in without a hammer, why the tapping had been so quiet. With sudden sickening clarity I found I could imagine the suited man clubbing the nails in with his fists, smashing them in with his forehead and grinning while he did it. Oh Jesus.

I walked downstairs again. Every single window. Even

the ones that were too small to climb through. Then as I stood in the kitchen amidst the growing piles, the pounding on the back door started. There was no way I could get out of the house. I couldn't stop it. This time it was going over all the way and taking me with it. And they were going to smash their way in to come along for the ride. To get me. I listened, watching the rubbish, as the pounding got louder and louder.

It's still getting louder, and I can tell from the sound that some of the planks are beginning to give way. The house stopped balancing long ago, and the change is coming on more quickly. The kitchen looks like a bomb site and there are an awful lot of spiders in there now. Eventually I left them to it and came through the hall into here, only making one or two wrong turnings. Into the living room.

And that's where I am now, just sitting and waiting. There is nothing I can do about the change, nothing. I can't get out. I can't stop them getting in.

But there is one thing I can do. I'm going to stay here, in the living room. I can see small shadows now, gathering in corners and darting out from under the chairs, and it's quite dark down by the end wall. The wall itself seems less important now, less substantial, less of a barrier. And I think I can hear the sound of running water somewhere far away, and smell the faintest hint of dark and lush vegetation.

I won't let them get me. I'll wait, in the gathering darkness here in the living room, listening to the coming of the night sounds, feeling a soft breeze on my face and sensing the room opening out as the walls shade away, as I sit here quietly in the dark warm air. And then I'll get up and start walking, walking out into the dark land, into the jungle and amidst the trees that stand all around behind the darkness, smelling the greenness that surrounds me and hearing the gentle river off somewhere to the right. And I'll feel happy walking away into the night, and maybe far away I'll meet whatever makes the growling sounds I begin to hear in the distance and we'll sit together by running water and be at peace in the darkness.

HORROR: 100 BEST BOOKS

STEPHEN JONES & KIM NEWMAN

'Horror is the branch of literature most often concerned with going too far . . .'
Ramsey Campbell

Who are the writers who do it best? Which are the books that the professionals really rate? What stories send icy fingers of fear up and down the spines of those who create dark dreams for a living?

100 of the world's top creators of horror were asked to write about their all-time favourite works of horror: from classic to contemporary, famous frighteners to newer nightmares lurking on the bookshelf.

The result was both fascinating and entertaining, and while such authors as Stephen King, Clive Barker, Peter Straub, Dan Simmons and many others worked and dissected, the full, disturbing range of horror fiction took shape . . .

'A book about the best work in the field by, arguably, its best writers . . . fascinating'
Fear

'A marvellous gathering . . . Highly recommended'
Locus

Winner of the Horror Writers of America Bram Stoker Award

HODDER AND STOUGHTON PAPERBACKS

NIGHT SHIFT

STEPHEN KING

A collection of horror stories that includes 'Children of the Corn', NIGHT SHIFT is a shudderingly detailed map of the dark places that lie behind our waking, rational world.

These are tales to invade and paralyse the mind as the safe light of day is infiltrated by the creeping, peopled shadows of night. As you read, the clutching fingers of terror brush lightly across the nape of the neck, reach round from behind to clutch and lock themselves, white-knuckled, around the throat.

This is the horror of ordinary people and everyday objects that become strangely altered; a world where nothing is ever quite what it seems, where the familiar and friendly lure and deceive. A world where madness and blind panic become the only reality.

HODDER AND STOUGHTON PAPERBACKS

BY BIZARRE HANDS

JOE LANSDALE

Joe R. Lansdale comes from Texas.

He has a mean imagination, a disturbing line in irony, a fine way with words and Award-winning habits.

'The genre's most interesting stylist . . . with a healthy sense of black humour and moral outrage'
New York Times

Life in his stories is short, brutish and full of the sort of folks you hope won't move in next door – let alone into your mind.

'A flavour unique in dark fantasy, a taste to be savoured, a book to be read'
Locus

Joe Lansdale will stop you in your tracks, make you wince. And make you think.

'Read any book or story by Joe Lansdale and pretty soon you gasp with astonishment'
Skeleton Crew

'A master story teller'
Fear

HODDER AND STOUGHTON PAPERBACKS

Other titles available from
New English Library paperbacks